MW01199944

PROTECTED BY THE COWBOY

A CONTEMPORARY CHRISTIAN ROMANCE

BLACKWATER RANCH
BOOK FOUR

MANDI BLAKE

Protected by the Cowboy
Blackwater Ranch Book Four
By Mandi Blake

Copyright © 2021 Mandi Blake
All Rights Reserved

No part of this book may be used or reproduced in any manner whatsoever without written permission, except in the case of brief quotations embedded in critical articles and reviews. The unauthorized reproduction or distribution of this copyrighted work is illegal. No part of this book may be scanned, uploaded or distributed via the Internet or any other means, electronic or print, without the author's permission.

This book is a work of fiction. The names, characters, places, and incidents are products of the writer's imagination or have been used fictitiously and are not to be construed as real. Any resemblance to persons, living or dead, actual events, locale or organizations is entirely coincidental. The author does not have any control over and does not assume any responsibility for third-party websites or their content.

Scripture quotations are from The ESV® Bible (The Holy Bible, English Standard Version®), copyright © 2001 by Crossway, a publishing ministry of Good News Publishers. Used by permission. All rights reserved. https://www.esv.org/resources/esv-global-study-bible/copyright-page/

Published in the United States of America
Cover Designer: Amanda Walker PA & Design Services
Editor: Editing Done Write
Ebook ISBN: 978-1-953372-03-1
Paperback ISBN: 978-1-953372-05-5

CONTENTS

CHAPTER 1
LANEY

"Please, please, please, please, please." The seat belt tightened against Laney's chest as she leaned into the steering wheel. The low fuel alarm beeped again.

"I said please!" she screamed above the road noise.

The ranch she was looking for had to be nearby. She'd checked the map and address before leaving the last rest stop, and she hadn't passed much of anything in the last five minutes.

Laney scanned the open road ahead. No landmarks. No signs.

"Come on, Ruby. You can do it." She brushed her hand over the dusty dashboard. Laney's old car, Ruby, had seen better days ten years ago. She'd named the old clunker before the rich red had faded to more of a rust color.

She'd spotted a truck parked on the side of the road in the distance when the alarm sounded again, and Ruby began to decelerate. Laney pressed on the pedal, but the needle on her speedometer was falling to the left. The needle on the fuel gauge danced as if looking for gas. "No!"

A sneaky tear slid down her cheek, and out of frustration, she quickly swiped it away. "Ow!" How could she forget about the bruise? It had pulsed painfully all night. Devin had gotten one shot at her, and he'd made it count.

Laney steered the car to the right until the passenger side came to rest in the tall grass lining the road. She banged her palm against the steering wheel and yelled, "Devin!"

Unfortunately, her fury couldn't touch him from here. She'd left Cheyenne and Devin early this morning, and she hoped to never lay eyes on either of them again.

She unlatched her seatbelt and leaned her forehead against the top of the steering wheel. If she blocked out everything and thought hard enough, she could forget about being stranded on the side of the road in the middle of nowhere.

The right side of her face burned where Devin's fist had landed last night. There was probably a broken bone hiding behind the dark-blue swelling, but there wasn't anything she could do about it. She didn't even have the money to buy cheap makeup to cover it up.

She was glad he'd only hit her once, but she really wished she'd seen it coming. She should've ducked faster.

A tapping on her window startled her, and she jerked up from the steering wheel. A man wearing a nice suit and a cowboy hat stood beside her car. The wide brim shadowed his eyes. He raised his hands and took a step back.

She pressed the button to roll the window down just enough to find out what he wanted.

"You need some help?" His voice was gruff, but he didn't look like the kind of guy to rough up women. She wasn't even sure how to tell which men were capable of violence and which ones weren't. It would be great if they came with a mark or a sign or something. Then she could have avoided Devin before he'd trapped her in a life she didn't want.

Laney wasn't sure if she wanted to laugh or cry, but either response would be an affirmative answer to his question. She studied him, wondering if she could trust this random man on the side of the road in the middle of nowhere. She had a painful reminder on her face of what trusting a man would get her, and she didn't want to make the same mistake twice.

The man tilted his head slightly. By the time she realized he was inspecting her bruise, it was too late.

He'd already gotten a good look at her face. She turned her head to look out the windshield at the road ahead. That truck parked beside the road in the distance must be his.

"Hey, are you okay?" he asked, his voice gentler this time.

The honest answer was no, but she wasn't about to admit it. She nodded her head slowly, wondering how she'd gotten so lost. Not on the road, but in life. Most adults in their mid-twenties were at least on the path to a career or a family. Laney was stranded on a rural road looking for a ranch where she may or may not get a housekeeping job.

"I'm looking for Blackwater Ranch." If he was a local, surely he could point her in the right direction.

The man turned to study the road ahead—the path her car refused to take her—then he turned his attention back to her. "Looks like you made it."

Laney squinted against the blinding sun as she looked for the ranch. "Where?"

He pointed to the truck up ahead. "I was putting up the sign. That's the entrance."

She nodded, trying to figure out how Ruby had timed her rest so perfectly.

The man cleared his throat. "What are you looking for at Blackwater?"

Great. He thought she was a trespasser. "I saw a job listing for a housekeeper position. I'd like to apply."

The man rubbed a hand over the back of his neck, then ran his fingers inside the collar of his shirt. "I doubt you'll get an interview today. Everyone is tied up with the wedding."

Her shoulders sank. A wedding. That explained why he was wearing a crisp suit. It didn't have the tailored look that Devin had used to fool her into thinking he was a respectable man, but this guy's suit didn't need alterations. It fit him well. She turned away before she let another man with a pretty face trick her into signing her life away.

What was she going to do until tomorrow? She hadn't seen a hotel in the last thirty miles. Not only that, she had no gas to get her there. She wasn't a fan of sleeping in the car.

The man tucked his hands into his pockets. "You want me to take a look at your car?"

He was studying her closer now, and she knew what he was seeing—her unwashed hair, swollen face, and bloodshot eyes. She'd avoided the mirror all morning and hoped she could land a job based on her work ethic, despite her haggard appearance.

He, on the other hand, looked strikingly handsome all clean shaven in a suit. He definitely had his act together. What would that be like?

She sucked in a deep breath through her nose. *Here goes nothing.*

"I don't think you need to. It's out of gas." If her cheeks weren't already blue, they'd be turning pink.

He probably thought she was irresponsible for letting the tank run dry. Actually, she hadn't had a choice, so the joke was on him. She had a few dollars to her name, and she needed it to last much longer than it was capable.

The man removed his hands from his pockets and shifted his weight. "I'm Micah Harding, the ranch manager." He tilted his head toward the truck in the distance. "I'll bring the fuel truck."

"Oh, thank you. I'll pay you back... soon." She wasn't sure *when* that would be, but soon was a relative term.

He raised a hand. "No need. I'll be right back."

Micah didn't waste any time turning back to the truck, and Laney wished he'd asked her to tag along. Sticking with the kind stranger seemed much safer than sitting in a stalled car on the side of the road.

She twisted in her seat to scan the road behind her. It was silly. No one was after her. Devin had probably already found someone to replace her. She locked the door and was about to roll up the window when she heard the man speak.

"You want to come with me?"

Laney jerked the keys from the ignition and jumped from the car. She took a few seconds to lock the door with her key before jogging to catch up with Micah.

He waited for her before resuming his steady

walk. He kept his attention on the road ahead. "I didn't catch your name."

She looked over her shoulder, but the only thing in sight was Ruby, the open road, and clear blue sky. "Oh, it's Laney." *Shoot.* She'd planned to use a fake name. Oh, well. It was too late now. "Laney Parker."

Micah didn't look at her as they walked side-by-side. "You from around here?"

Oh no. The interrogation. If she clammed up just chatting with the ranch manager, she was bound to flub the interview. She remembered her dad's coaching when she was young about how to talk to the police. Tell as much of the truth as you can without giving away the farm. Answer the question using as few words as possible. Don't let your emotions get out of hand.

"Um. No." There. Truth, but no cherry on top.

"Where are you staying?"

More questions. Maybe she should have stayed in the car. "Well, nowhere right now."

Micah turned his head and gave her a questioning look.

"I was going to see how the interview went and then find a place." Truth—in part. She really hadn't thought about where she would stay. She didn't have the money to afford anything. Devin took almost all of her pay to cover the rent each month. The realization settled in, and she focused on controlling her breathing. Going back to Cheyenne was out of the question. Where *was* she going to stay?

When they reached the truck, Micah walked around to the passenger side and opened the door for her. Laney kept her gaze on him as she slid into the pickup truck. It was new and fancy and huge. She rubbed her hands over the soft leather on the seat beside her.

Micah settled into the driver's seat and removed his suit jacket before shifting into gear. His arms were thick and strained against the white dress shirt. She averted her gaze and swallowed hard. Devin's punch had hurt bad enough. She'd hate to find out what kind of damage a man like Micah could do to her.

The truck had been left running, so it was warm inside the cab. Laney tucked her hands between her knees and leaned against the door. She felt small and weak sitting beside this man who took up more than his allotted space in the truck.

She cleared her throat and fidgeted, pushing her hair behind her ear. "Thanks for helping me out. I know this isn't the best first impression."

Micah nodded. "No problem. How did you hear about the job?"

A big house came into view, and Laney leaned forward in her seat. There were a dozen vehicles parked in front of the two-story wooden house. "I read about it on the website."

Micah didn't ask any more questions as they drove past the big house with all the cars. He steered the truck past one barn and toward another until they came to a stop. He motioned for her to follow him as he got out of the truck, so she scrambled out to catch up with him.

The inside of the barn was massive. No less than a dozen big machines filled the covered area. He raised a garage door on one side of the barn, and light flooded the dusty building.

Micah picked up an opaque jar and tipped it over. A handful of keys tumbled into his hand, and he selected one before putting the rest back into the jar.

He jerked his head, indicating she should follow him. He opened the passenger door of a white truck with a huge box on the flatbed. She slid into the older truck and waited in the silence as he made his way around to get in on the driver's side. He started the engine and cut a suspicious glance her way before shifting into gear. She'd bet her first paycheck that he was going to move that jar of keys before the day was over.

The way back to her car was quiet, except for the humming of the engine, and she fidgeted in her seat. She'd changed her mind about his questions. She preferred interrogation to this silence.

Micah parked the fuel truck beside her car and

got out. Laney slipped from the truck, feeling help-less as he pumped the gas into her empty tank.

Laney folded her arms over her chest. "Thanks again for this. I'm sorry to put you through the trouble."

Micah looked up at her, and then turned away just as quickly. "It's not a problem." He cleared his throat and kept his attention on the pump. When the tank was full, he rested the pump in its place on the truck and twisted the cap back on her tank.

Then he stood to his full height, shoulders back and chin up, before asking, "Where are you headed?"

Laney felt her throat tighten. Micah had already told her she wasn't getting an interview today, but where did that leave her? She had no idea where to go next, and the realization coupled with his ques-tioning was threatening to push her over an emotional edge.

"I think I'll head into town and see if I can find a hotel. Any suggestions?" The question was all for show. She didn't have the money to afford a hotel room.

Micah tugged at his collar. "The only thing around here is the Kellerman Hotel."

Laney nodded and stuck her hands into her back pockets. "Thanks again. I'll come back tomorrow and see if I can get an interview."

Micah looked at her car and back toward the

ranch. "You can stay in one of the wranglers' cabins tonight if you want. We could do the interview in the morning after breakfast."

She was afraid to move or even breathe. "Really? That would be great." She wasn't sure how much they'd charge for the overnight stay, but she'd settle that debt, as well as the one with Micah, as soon as she got her first paycheck.

If she got the job.

He rubbed the back of his neck. "It's not much. No TV or internet, but it has water and electricity."

Laney felt her lips tugging into a smile. "I don't mind. Thanks again."

Micah's own flat expression began to change into something friendlier. "You're welcome. Follow me."

She jumped into her car and started the engine. Ruby's loud rumble filled the air. "Thanks, girl. I knew we'd make it."

Laney drove slowly behind Micah's truck as he turned to the right just before the big, wooden house. They'd gone left before. Soon, a row of replicated cabins came into view. They dotted the tree line for a quarter of a mile, evenly spaced and equally quaint.

Micah's truck came to a stop in front of the farthest cabin, and Laney parked Ruby beside it. She stared at the small, wooden house, unable to understand how her life had changed so much in the last twenty-four hours. The cozy cabin looked nothing like her place in Cheyenne.

The slamming of Micah's truck door startled her out of her daydream. She took a deep breath and stepped out into the cold Wyoming wind.

CHAPTER 2
MICAH

Micah rounded the front of the truck and stepped up beside Laney as she pulled a duffel bag out of the backseat. Before he could say anything, she turned around and let out a sharp yelp, jumping six inches backward. She lost her balance and fell back against the car.

"Ouch." She tucked her elbow in and rubbed it. "You scared me. I didn't know you were behind me."

Micah reached for the duffel bag and rested the strap over his shoulder. "I didn't mean to scare you. Just wanted to help you carry your things."

Laney brushed a hand over her scattering hair, trying and failing to wrangle it from the wind. "Thank you."

He tilted his head toward the cabin. "I'll show you around and then let you get settled in."

The soft crunch of her steps on the dirt behind

him was comforting. Laney Parker didn't look much older than a high schooler, and when she wasn't speaking, he could almost imagine she'd been a dream. An intense quietness settled around her, but he'd have to be blind not to notice her or the bruise on her face.

She was a puzzle wrapped in a mystery at the center of a labyrinth, and he had a million questions for the woman who'd shown up at Blackwater unannounced. The last time that happened, Asher had found the woman he married.

Haley had shocked the entire ranch when she'd turned up a few months ago, but Laney could sneak in under the radar if it weren't for the bruise on her face.

His hand began to sweat against the strap of the duffel bag as he stepped onto the porch and opened the door for Laney to enter first. She paused just before the threshold, and her gaze darted around them. What was she afraid of here?

Worry swirled in his middle. Was she afraid of him? He'd never hurt a woman, but she didn't know that.

Micah stepped into the cabin and turned on the light. Laney followed him inside, keeping her arms tucked closely across her chest. His attention was drawn to the bruise covering the right side of her face, and something dark and angry stirred inside him. Violence rarely crossed his mind, but he had the uncontrollable urge to break a few bones in his hand against the face of the person who'd given her that bruise, and he would bet his last paycheck that it had been a man. She leaned away from him and kept a safe distance.

Laney backed up to the wall and studied the room. "This is nice."

Micah huffed a half-laugh and felt the corners of his mouth tug. "It's not much, but it's a free place to stay." He pointed a thumb at the lonely couch in the center of the room facing a small stone fireplace. "This is the living area. The kitchen is over there, but it isn't stocked." He pointed at the various places in the small cabin, ticking off the obvious rooms. "That door is the bathroom, and that one is the bedroom."

She stuck her hands in her back pockets and shifted her weight from one foot to the other. "Thanks again. It really is nice. I appreciate this."

What was it about this woman that made him want to cater to her? Her expression was a mix between shattered hope and admiration, and it was tearing him up.

He set the duffel bag on the couch and tried to think of things she'd need tonight. "Well, I'll grab some firewood and be back in a little while. Feel free to settle in. I'll let the owners know about the interview in the morning."

Laney twisted her fingers together. "Thank you. I'm sorry to be such a burden."

Micah studied her again, wondering what made her think taking a little time to help her out was a sacrifice. "You're not a burden." His parents had taught him to be charitable to a fault, and all the Hardings had grown up helping the other families nearby.

She chewed her bottom lip and kept her gaze on the floor at his feet. Did she always wear her worries on her face?

"I'll be back soon. Here's my number if you need anything." He pulled a plain business card from his wallet and handed it to her. He tipped his hat and walked out the door that creaked as it closed behind him.

His thoughts were a blur of questions as he drove to the small storage shed behind the main house where they kept the firewood. They'd cleaned out all of the cabin chimneys recently when the family had met about the expansion of the ranch. With the bed and breakfast booming in its first season, they hoped to hire a few more hands to cater to the tourist side of the business. Haley was doing a great job of welcoming guests and keeping things running, but they desperately needed to hire a housekeeper before the bed and breakfast over-whelmed her.

Micah stacked a few pieces of firewood into the floorboard of the fuel truck. The sun would be sinking behind the distant Tetons soon, and everyone would be sitting down to yet another catered meal to celebrate Asher and Haley's wedding.

He made a quick decision and stepped inside the main house. The back rooms were quieter, but the chatter of the crowd grew louder as he drew closer to the meeting room. The reception had been at the church, but most of the guests had been invited back to the ranch for supper. Haley liked to be settled in before dark, so the celebration was relocated.

Slipping in through the kitchen, Micah grabbed a disposable plate and began heaping food from the serving counter onto it. His stomach was growling, but he could wait until he'd delivered Laney's supper and firewood before coming back to pick at what was left.

"Hey, stranger!"

Micah tried not to wince at the high-pitched voice beside him. "Olivia." He tried to rein in the harshness of his voice.

"I've been looking for you." She rested a mani-cured hand on his arm. "I saw you in the wedding. You look so handsome."

He hadn't seen Olivia Lawrence in a while, but not much had changed. He'd agreed to be her date to her senior prom ten years ago, and she'd acted as if they had a deep history ever since. If he'd known she would put so much meaning behind the date, he'd have skipped it altogether.

"Thanks. You look nice too." He gave her half a second of his attention. Olivia *did* look nice. She was wearing a modest dress with her short, dark hair that was sleek and straight. Her friendly smile was genuine. He knew that much. He'd known Olivia Lawrence his whole life, and she didn't have an unkind bone in her body.

Her hand slipped from his arm as he scooped a ladle of gravy onto a heap of mashed potatoes. He'd have to be careful not to spill gravy all over everything between here and Laney's cabin.

Micah sighed. When had he started thinking of it as Laney's cabin? She'd been here for half an hour, and he was already giving her stock in the ranch.

Soft music filled the meeting room, and Olivia turned to the open space on the far side of the room. Micah and Lucas had moved the tables aside to make room for the guests to dance this evening.

Micah turned to see his brother, Asher, dancing with his new bride. Micah hadn't ever felt the itch to draw attention to himself, but he couldn't say the same for his brothers. He was happy hanging out on the sidelines while the other Hardings stole the show.

"Will you dance with me?" Olivia asked tentatively.

Micah cleared his throat, hoping to soften his words. "Um..."

"Not right this second. Maybe after you finish

eating?" Her words were so hopeful, tilting high at the end.

"I have a few things to do before I can hang out. I don't want to make a promise I can't keep, but I'll try to be back in time."

Olivia's thin lips tugged wide, but it was the smile in her eyes that had guilt rushing up his spine. Did it matter if he danced with her if his heart wasn't in it? He knew it wasn't good for either of them if he led her on.

"I'm sorry. Things are really busy right now, and I—"

Olivia held up a hand to halt his words. "I know. You've had the same answer every time I've run into you since high school. It's always a busy time." The joy from only moments ago fell from her face, replaced by a brave, fake grin. "I'll catch you some other time."

She patted his shoulder as she stepped around him and made her way back into the crowd of people.

He'd been honest with her, but why did he still feel like a jerk? He rubbed a hand over his face and grabbed a handful of napkins. He ducked back into the kitchen without anyone noticing. He liked being able to come and go as he pleased. His brothers, Asher and Lucas, couldn't go anywhere without attracting attention. But no one expected Micah to chat about the weather or gripe about the short hay season. No one expected him to do anything except get the job done, and he was glad to do it.

In the kitchen, he covered the plate with aluminum foil, making sure the edges were tight. The last thing he wanted was to bring Laney gravy-less potatoes.

A minute later, he balanced the plate, plasticware wrapped in napkins, and a bottle of water as he stepped out into the twilight. He still needed to hang the new sign at the road, but he could wake up early to get it done before breakfast.

He held a hand over the plate as the truck pitched and dipped across the uneven lane to the cabins. Delivering supper was a lot more tedious than hauling cattle.

Micah steadied the plate on one hand and piled the extras on top before tucking the water bottle under his arm. He could be overstepping. What if she planned to go into town for supper?

He shook that thought out of his head when he remembered her empty gas tank. She'd passed a fuel station when she turned onto the main road running by the ranch, but she hadn't stopped. He was having a tough time understanding why someone would pass a station knowing their fuel was low.

He stopped at the door and raised a fist to knock, but an unfamiliar fear made him pause. The only logical reason she would have run out of gas was if she didn't have the money to pay.

Micah rapped his knuckles against the worn wood and scratched at the bristle on his cheek. Thinking about a woman running out of gas on the side of the road without money sent a cold sweat running down his back.

The door creaked open, and Laney stuck her head into the narrow opening. "Hey." She opened the door wide, allowing him inside.

He thrust the plate balanced on his hand toward her. "I brought you some supper. My brother got married today, and they're having a party at the main house."

Laney eyed the plate but didn't reach for it.

Micah shrugged, hoping to downplay his gesture. "It was catered, so I fixed you a plate." He held out the bottle of water in his other hand, silently pleading with her to take it.

She slowly reached for the plate and water, and Micah released a tense breath when the offering had passed hands.

He stuck his hands in his pockets, unsure what to do with them. "I'll go get the firewood."

Forcing himself not to run from the room, he controlled his pace as he stepped outside. Everything he didn't know about Laney was putting him on edge. Indecision gripped him. Had he made a mistake in bringing her here?

Micah stacked the firewood in his arms and walked back inside in a fog of worries. He closed the door, blocking out the cold evening air.

Laney stood beside the round four-seater table in the kitchen. The plate of food and water sat untouched.

Micah paused, waiting for her to sit, but she didn't.

"You can start eating if you want. It'll take me a minute to get the fire going. Then I'll get out of your way."

Laney eased into one of the old, wooden chairs but didn't move to uncover the food.

He turned to the task of starting the fire, hoping to quell his urge to push her to eat. When he'd finished propping the wood in the fireplace, she still hadn't opened the food. He hadn't heard the crinkle of the aluminum foil, and he could feel his blood pressure rising. He'd been in this monkey suit all day, and the back stretched tight across his shoulders as he leaned over the fireplace.

When the fire crawled up the sides of the split wood, he stood and tucked his hands into his coat pocket. "I left a few more pieces you can put on in the night if you need to." He tilted his head toward the card bearing his phone number that lay on the table next to the unopened plate of food. "Just call me if you need anything."

Laney stood. "Thank you... for everything. What

time should I be ready for the interview in the morning?"

"I'll pick you up at seven for breakfast."

"Breakfast?" Laney asked, tilting her head slightly.

Micah rubbed the back of his neck. "Everyone eats breakfast together. Then we meet about our tasks for the day before heading out."

"Oh." The small word seemed to die as it passed her lips.

"You don't have to eat breakfast with everyone, but you're welcome to join. My parents will be in the interview. Haley might be there too. She's been running things with the bed and breakfast. You can meet them."

Why was he trying to talk her into breakfast? Better yet, why was she hesitant to do any of the things he advised? Her cheeks were on the gaunt side, and his jaw twitched as his teeth ground against each other. He couldn't tell much about the rest of her, but he had a feeling the baggy sweater was hanging on a skeleton.

She shifted her weight from one side to the other and asked, "Do you think the bruise will make everyone uncomfortable? I don't really have a good explanation."

He could name at least two people who were going to feel uncomfortable through all of this—him and Laney.

"Don't worry about it. I'll let them know who you are and that you're being interviewed after breakfast. The questions won't start until then."

Laney tucked her arms in closer around her chest. "Will they listen to you?"

The chuckle had escaped before he'd been able to contain it, but he forced his lips not to turn up in a smile. She'd been serious when she'd asked if his younger brothers and employees would take him seriously. "They'll listen." He wasn't afraid to kick any of his brothers in the seat of the pants if they asked for it. Maybe not Hunter. Micah would think twice before throwing hands with his cousin.

"Okay," Laney whispered. "Thank you. I'll be ready."

Micah tipped his hat and walked out. He needed a moment of peace without worries for Laney screaming in his head.

The main house was lit up from the inside like a lantern against the darkening sky, and he had no desire to go back and mingle with the wedding party.

Knowing they wouldn't miss him, Micah left the fuel truck parked in front of the cabin Laney would be staying in tonight and walked the thirty feet to his own cabin. Once inside, he hung his hat on the rack and rested his back against the cold wood of the door. He clasped his hands in front of his face and leaned his forehead against his knuckles.

He hadn't been able to think straight since that mysterious woman landed on his ranch, and he had no idea how he was going to be able to put in a full work day tomorrow without worrying about her. At least he was guaranteed to spend a good part of the morning with her. They had breakfast and an interview bright and early.

He'd never been twisted up over a woman before, but Laney was different. She kept looking over her shoulder like it wasn't safe to relax, and she seemed eager for the interview in the morning. They could use an extra set of hands around the main house.

The fact that she was beautiful didn't help matters. And while he hadn't been sucker punched by a gorgeous woman in a while, Laney was attractive in an unexpected way. Her hair wasn't styled, and she hadn't worn a stitch of makeup, even to cover the bruise.

But those eyes. They were curious, and his stomach had tumbled off a high-rise every time she'd glanced his way.

He'd have all morning with her, but after that, what was he going to do about the mysterious stranger in the cabin next to his?

CHAPTER 3
LANEY

Laney squeezed her eyes closed when her alarm sounded the next morning and immediately regretted it. Pain throbbed in her cheek, and she reached up to touch it.

She turned off her alarm and writhed in the bed. The pain had kept her up most of the night, and she'd been afraid of oversleeping. Everything was riding on her interview this morning.

Groaning, she sat up in bed and wondered how she would make it through breakfast without blowing chunks. The pain was nauseating, and she needed to make a good impression this morning.

Laney eyed her royal-blue duffel bag and focused on sucking deep breaths in through her nose. The Oak Hill High School bag had been with her through half a dozen moves since she'd graduated. She'd named it Ollie after the yeti mascot branded on the side, and he'd been right beside her through some of the worst times of her life.

She sighed. What did it say about her that her most trusted confidant was a getaway bag? If she'd been born into a better family, she'd have sought out a therapist years ago.

On the other hand, if she'd had parents who cared one iota about her, she might not be naming inanimate objects.

Laney stood and stretched her arms above her head before grabbing a handful of clothes and tiptoeing into the bathroom. The small space was oddly comforting, despite the frigid morning. The fire had gone out in the night, but she'd been too tired to revive it.

She took longer than usual in the shower. Devin wasn't around to yell at her, and she scrubbed her body with her eyes closed, savoring the silence.

After she'd dressed and brushed her teeth, she wrapped her wet hair in a tight bun on the top of her head. She'd need her hair out of the way while she worked today, but the sight of the bruise in the mirror had her stomach sinking. There wasn't a way to hide it, but that didn't make it any easier to lift her chin. Sometimes, the shadows weighed too much, and it was easier to succumb to the darkness.

She stepped back into the bedroom and tossed her dirty clothes beside Ollie. How long would it be before she was packing up again with her trusty duffel bag?

Laney leaned her shoulder against the wall and rested her head against the cold wood. "I hope we get to stay here again tonight."

Ollie didn't answer, but thankfully, neither did Devin. It had been almost a full day since he'd spewed hateful names at her. If her cheek wasn't giving her such a fit, she'd probably be singing with the morning songbirds.

Laney grabbed her phone from the nightstand. There were dozens of missed calls from Devin and thirty-six texts.

She tried to swallow, but it felt like someone had stuffed cotton in her throat. She plugged the beat-up phone in to charge and left it in the bedroom. The only person she'd be hearing from was Devin, and she needed to focus on getting the job here today.

In the kitchen, she turned on the tap and filled her cupped hand with water. She'd finished off the bottle Micah had brought her after she scarfed down the delicious dinner, and she hadn't found a glass in any of the cabinets.

She wiped her mouth on the sleeve of her shirt and spotted the card Micah had left on the table. She'd never had a lifeline before, but a spark of hope kindled in her heart. She wanted to believe Micah had been sincere when he'd offered his help last night, but it went against everything she'd experienced in the last twenty-six years. Men weren't helpful.

Laney chewed on her thumbnail as she stared at the card. The last thing she needed was to become dependent on another man.

But Micah was *kind*.

She jumped when a knock at the door rattled the perfect silence.

Her heartbeat was still pounding in her throat when she reached the door. Devin wasn't here. It was only Micah.

She grabbed her coat from the rack and opened the door.

The cold morning air wasn't nearly as shocking as the handsome man standing on the porch. The crisp suit he'd worn yesterday had been replaced by a thick coat, faded jeans, and dirty work boots, but Laney was now convinced that Micah Harding looked good in anything.

"Morning." His mouth tugged to one side in a half-smile.

Hundreds of men had catcalled, whistled, and manhandled her at the bar where she'd worked for Devin, but no one had ever gifted her a sweet smile the way Micah did.

"Good morning." Oh, what a good morning it was.

Micah held out a fist between them and opened it. In his palm sat two white pills.

"It's for the pain. You looked pretty uncomfortable yesterday."

"What are they?" she asked.

"Aspirin."

Laney stared at the pills in his hand and fought the urge to cry. She'd never wanted anything in her life the way she wanted that relief, and he was giving it to her.

"Thank you." The words were scratchy as she pushed them past her tightening throat. With shaky hands, she took the pills and slipped them into the front pocket of her jeans.

"You ready?" Micah asked.

Laney nodded and followed him to the truck where he opened the door for her and shut it behind her when she'd settled in. What kind of alternate reality had she stepped into? She'd been working twelve hour days at Devin's bar, Dive In, for years, and not once had a man opened a door for her.

Neither of them spoke as they drove to the big house she'd seen yesterday. Nerves swarmed in her middle like bees as they drew closer.

"Don't be nervous. Everyone here will be nice to you." Micah's words were clipped and matter-of-fact, but they rang with truth.

She nodded, scanning the ranch for any sign of trouble. She hadn't been able to shake the fear that she wasn't out of the woods yet, and old habits die hard.

A long-haired black-and-white dog ran out from behind a nearby shed and followed them until they parked in front of the big house.

"Is that your dog?" Laney asked.

"That's Dixie. I guess she's everyone's dog." He shrugged, opened the door, and stepped out.

Laney opened the door on her side of the truck, and the dog barked and jumped.

Micah was beside her within seconds. "She won't bite. She's just excited to see you."

Laney slipped from her seat and held out a hand to the dog. The only dogs she'd been around were more like guard dogs and not to be touched.

Dixie sniffed the hand and ducked her head beneath it, brushing Laney's hand over the black patch behind her ears.

"She seems nice," Laney said as she crouched next to Dixie.

"She's a good one," Micah said. "Probably the most reliable worker on the ranch."

Laney smiled, and the tug in her cheek made her wince. She wanted to get inside and take the pills with her breakfast, but she had a greater urge to snuggle the friendly dog.

"Hey, Dixie. It's nice to meet you."

Dixie wallowed in Laney's affection. She'd always wanted a pet, mainly a dog or a horse, but her parents hadn't let her entertain the idea of either. They didn't have the money and hadn't wanted the responsibility.

They hadn't wanted the responsibility of a daughter either, but they were free of their obligation now.

"Everyone else will be here soon. Do you want to meet my parents before the crowd shows up?"

Laney stood and jerked her head to him. "How many people are there? Why would I meet your parents?" She'd known there would be a lot to take in this morning, but she felt as if she'd just been thrown into a whirlpool.

Micah stuck his hands in his pockets. "They're the owners. I'm the manager. We'll meet with them for the interview after breakfast."

"Oh." Laney pushed the word from her mouth and nodded. "Okay."

She really wanted to stay outside with Dixie. It sounded like a much better idea than going inside to meet people.

Micah toed off his boots and set them against the wall beside the door. "Our boots are usually dirty, so Mama wants us to take them off. You can leave yours on."

Laney followed Micah inside and swallowed a gasp. The room was huge and welcoming with plenty of light and windows that framed pictures of the dawn beyond.

"This way. Mom and Dad will be in the kitchen."

Micah led the way, and she scanned the open room as she followed. He opened a door for her to enter, and she slipped past him. A masculine scent of clean pine filled her senses, and she breathed deeper.

Once inside the kitchen, the smell of cooked bacon was comforting. Laney wrapped her arms around her middle, hoping her stomach wouldn't growl.

A petite woman with slightly graying hair pulled into a bun atop her head stepped around the corner. Her smile was bright, but it quickly dimmed as she turned her attention to Laney. The woman rested the bowl she'd been carrying on the counter and wiped her hands on her apron.

"Good morning." She seemed at a loss for words as she tilted her head to the side and looked to Micah.

Laney hated the glaring bruise. The few people she'd seen since Devin laid it on her had been uncomfortable. She was self-conscious enough without an awkward elephant sitting on her face.

"Mom, this is Laney Parker. She's the one interviewing this morning. Laney, this is my mom, Anita Harding."

Anita's smile was back. "It's a pleasure to meet you. Everyone calls me Mama Harding. Micah told me you arrived yesterday. I'm sorry we weren't prepared for an interview."

"That's okay," Laney said. "I showed up unannounced." She picked at her fingernails and turned to Micah. "Micah told me I could stay in one of the cabins last night. I hope that's okay."

Mama Harding held out her arms and gently wrapped them around Laney's shoulders. She sucked in a startled breath as the woman's warmth seeped through her sweater.

"That's perfectly fine. It made sense, considering you'd just be coming back this morning."

Laney wrapped her arms gently around the woman just before she pulled back.

"I'm glad you're joining us for breakfast," Mama Harding said as she moved to pick up the bowl she'd been carrying before the introduction.

Heat burned in Laney's face. She'd have to meet more people soon, and she was already dying of embarrassment.

"Hey."

Laney lifted her head to Micah who'd whispered beside her.

"Would you feel more comfortable if we fixed our plates and ate in here?" he asked.

She considered the offer. Would it be cowardly if she said yes?

"It's okay if you want to sneak off and skip the breakfast meetings. It isn't required. You can meet them later if you get the job." Micah pushed his hands into his pockets. "I was just thinking you could relax a little before the interview."

The offer of a peaceful breakfast was too good to ignore. "I'd like that."

Micah tilted his head toward the door. "Let's get our food before everyone gets here."

Laney nodded and followed Micah to the big room they'd entered first. He handed her a plate at the beginning of a long serving counter filled with bowls and trays of food. Her mouth watered at the delicious smell, and she had to force herself not to pile food onto her plate.

Back in the kitchen, Micah pulled out a barstool beside an island and motioned for her to sit. He took the stool beside her and fidgeted a minute before clearing his throat. "I'd like to say grace."

Laney rested the fork back on her plate and felt embarrassment creeping up her neck. She had no idea what to do, so when he bowed his head, she did the same.

"Father, thank You for this food and the hands that prepared it. Please be with Laney this morning and fill her with peace and healing. In Jesus' name I pray. Amen."

Micah picked up the fork and used the side edge to cut into a biscuit covered in gravy, but Laney stared at the food on her plate. She'd never heard a real prayer before. She'd heard plenty of Devin's curses at God and others, but never a thankful prayer to God or a prayer asking for something.

Not only had it seemed sweet and genuine, but Micah had prayed for *her* when he could have prayed for himself. The logic confused her.

"You okay?" Micah asked.

Laney nodded quickly and picked up her fork. It was a great test of restraint not to shovel the food into her mouth. She'd been eating in a hurry for years now, and savoring her food now was a treat. Everything was delicious and full of flavor. By the time she'd finished, she felt full to bursting, and her insides were warm from the hot food.

Micah pushed his plate to the side and faced her. A few tense heartbeats passed before he spoke.

"I won't force you to tell me anything you don't want to, but I think I need to know how you got that bruise before we consider hiring you."

All of the oxygen left her lungs. Would she be killing her chances of getting the job before the interview even started if she told him the truth?

Micah's voice was softer as he added, "I just want to make sure you're not in any trouble, and we don't want trouble here either. I won't hold anything against you."

Laney swallowed her doubts. If she wanted a chance at getting the job here, she'd have to come clean.

CHAPTER 4
MICAH

Micah hated the scared expression on Laney's face. Hadn't he made her feel safe here? Her jumpy reactions upped the urgency to find out what kept her so hyper-alert. If she felt unsafe here, it was because of some outside force. Nothing here could hurt her.

Laney picked at her fingernails and bit her bottom lip. She lifted her head to face him. "I had a job at a bar, and one of the owners was my boyfriend. We had a customer who was well past drunk and causing some trouble, so I told him he was cut off for the night. My boyfriend didn't like that. Things got out of hand, and he hit me." She shrugged as if the events were expected. "I left the next morning when he went to work. I couldn't stay there anymore."

Micah nodded and rubbed a hand over his jaw.

The rage in his chest turned white-hot. He refused to let his mind wander to the torturous things he'd like to do to her boyfriend—well, her ex-boyfriend, if she'd left him with no intention of going back.

He forced out the words, "Had he hit you before?"

Laney shook her head. "That was the first time he'd hit me. He'd grabbed me a few times or shoved me against the wall, but that was the first real hit."

Micah leapt from the barstool, and the wooden legs rattled against the floor as it wobbled. "That's not okay, Laney. None of it is." It made his stomach turn, and her blatant telling of the violence was all wrong.

A boulder the size of Wyoming dropped in his stomach when her gaze met his. "I know. I knew it would happen again if I stayed."

"Where are you from?" Micah asked.

"Cheyenne."

Micah nodded. "Does he know you're here?"

"No." Laney shook her head. "I left a note that said I was quitting at the bar. I also said I was leaving town and not coming back."

"Good. What made you come here?" he asked.

She twisted her fingers, and her gaze dropped to the floor. "I don't know. I stopped at a library on my way out of town and searched for job openings. I'm not qualified for much. I don't have a degree or any training to speak of. I've been a waitress and a bar back, but that's about it. I ran across the job listing for the housekeeper here, and I thought it was a good idea to get out of Cheyenne." Her eyes turned glassy. "I almost didn't make it."

"So, that's why you ran out of gas?"

She lifted her head and blinked rapidly. "I thought if I could just get here, I could show you I can be the best worker. I don't have experience as a housekeeper, but I can learn anything, and I work hard."

"I have no doubt." Micah raised his hand to assure her. "You'll get your chance here. I don't think we've had applicants knocking down the door."

She relaxed a fraction. "Thank you. For everything. I wasn't prepared for the last twenty-four hours."

"I would say I get it, but I can't imagine what you've been through." He didn't want to dwell on those troublesome thoughts.

She raised her brows. "It's something I'd like to forget."

Micah reached for her empty plate. "I'll put these away, and we can wait in the den while everyone else finishes breakfast."

Laney grabbed their glasses and followed him to the sink where they left the dishes. In the den, her gaze darted to every wall, every surface, until her attention fell on the wall of shelves opposite the hearth.

"Wow." Awe filled her voice as her eyes widened. "It's like a library."

Micah chuckled. He'd grown used to the wall of books in the house he'd grown up in. His mother had read most of them aloud to him before he could read on his own. After he learned, he'd read many of them again.

"You like to read?" he asked.

Laney shrugged. "I don't know. I've never had much time to read."

Micah stepped up behind her as she admired the bounty of books. "Lots of choices here."

She flinched when he spoke and stepped to the side. He'd have to remember to give her space.

Laney ran her fingertips along the spine of a worn hardback. "It's overwhelming... thinking about all the words in these books. There are so many of them."

Micah rubbed his chin. "It's not so bad if you cut out the ones you don't like."

She turned to him and tilted her head. "What do you mean?"

"There are all kinds of books. Mystery, westerns, the classics. You probably won't like them all, so don't worry about those. Who has time to read books they don't like?"

Laney shrugged. "I never thought about it that way. I don't know what kind of books I would like."

He moved a step closer to her as she eyed a C.S.

Lewis classic. "I probably wouldn't start there. Lewis isn't an easy read."

Her eyes were bright when she turned to him. The sight of her stole his breath. He'd never been the type to get caught up in the sight of a woman, but he could stare at Laney all day.

"Hey, you two."

Micah jumped back at Haley's quick entrance. "We were just... talking about books." Why did he feel the need to explain their actions? He was allowed to be alone in a room with a woman.

Funny, he'd felt more at ease when he and Laney had been the only ones in the room. And from Laney's rigid stance, it seemed she did too.

"I'm Laney Parker." She stuck her hand out to Haley, but the smile on her face was guarded—no doubt waiting for Haley to notice the bruise.

Micah cleared his throat. Laney had beat him to the introduction. "Laney, this is Haley, my sister-in-law. She has pretty much taken over the bed and breakfast side of the ranch."

Haley reached for Laney's offered hand, but her welcoming smile dimmed when she noticed Laney's face. "It's nice to meet you. I just heard you'd be interviewing this morning." Haley tilted her head and raised an eyebrow. Her voice softened. "Are you okay?"

"I am. It's really not as bad as it looks," Laney explained.

Micah doubted her words were honest. He'd seen her winces throughout the morning, and each one had pricked at his heart like a needle sliding into a pincushion.

Haley shook Laney's hand and accepted her answer. "I'm glad. You've got a real shiner there."

Haley gestured to the sitting area. "You want to get comfortable? Silas and Anita will be here soon."

Micah followed Haley and Laney to the other side of the room where Laney chose a recliner that faced the couch and loveseat. Haley scooted to one side of the couch, while he sat rigid and alert on the loveseat. He wouldn't be able to relax until this interview was over, if then. Laney's unease was making him uncomfortable.

Micah's parents entered within seconds, and he felt his heart rate skyrocket. He knew Laney was getting the job today. He'd talked to his parents early this morning, and they'd already made a decision about her. She was willing to work, needed the job, and she was friendly, despite the glaring bruise that covered the side of her face.

Laney stood to greet the newcomers and held her chin high. What did it take to look strangers in the eye when no one saw past her marred face?

His mother gave Laney a welcoming smile and wrapped an arm around Micah's father.

"I'm Silas Harding. Welcome to Blackwater. Micah tells me you stayed in one of the wranglers' cabins last night. I'm sorry we didn't have a better room for you."

Mama Harding stepped up beside her husband. "We were celebrating Asher and Haley's wedding. They got married yesterday."

Haley beamed. "It's nice to be Haley Harding now."

"Congratulations," Laney said. "I'm sorry I intruded. I should have called ahead."

Mama Harding waved her hand. "It's no problem. I hope the cabin was okay. It was cold last night."

Laney's mouth tilted up on the left side—the one free of the bruise. "Micah made a fire. It was perfect. Thank you so much for letting me stay."

Mama Harding took a seat on the couch next to Silas. "You're welcome here. So, how did you hear about the job?"

Laney sat on the edge of the seat with her back straight. No one would guess she'd been beaten by a monster, left her job and home, ran out of gas on the side of the road, and slept in a stranger's cabin in the last twenty-four hours.

She tucked a stray strand of hair behind her ear. "I found the job listing online. I came from Cheyenne, but I thought a change of scenery might do me good."

Micah huffed. That was an understatement. She shouldn't have been anywhere near that man who didn't have the decency to keep his hands off a woman.

Micah clenched his jaw and tried to control his breathing. Each breath was quicker and shallower than the last. If he could get his hands on the guy who'd hit Laney—

"You'll love it here," Haley said. "The ranch is beautiful, and the people aren't too bad either." She winked at Micah as if they shared a secret.

"What about Cheyenne? Do you have family there?" Silas asked.

Laney shook her head. "No. I haven't seen my parents since I moved out when I was eighteen."

She shrugged as if it wasn't a big deal, but Micah detected a hint of pain in her eyes that ripped him open.

"No parents?" Haley asked as if the idea were incomprehensible to her.

"I mean, I have parents, but they don't care about me." Laney rubbed her knuckles in her lap but kept her gaze on Haley. "They weren't the best parents, and they were ready to get rid of me."

Micah rested his forehead in his hand. He didn't want to hear any more about her parents. Who could raise a kid and not care about her? It wasn't something he could understand.

Who could ever be close to Laney and consider hitting her? Only a monster—a monster Micah wanted to introduce to his fist.

His mother leaned forward to pat Laney's knee. "We're all family here."

Moisture filled Laney's eyes, and Micah tucked his chin again. He wanted to get out of this room. He knew there was injustice and cruelty in the world, but it hadn't ever come knocking at his door. Seeing Laney unbroken by the rough hand she'd been dealt made him want to right all the wrongs.

"I don't have a resume of stellar jobs, but I'm a hard worker and will do anything you need me to do," Laney said in her defense.

"That's good. We have a lot to do here. We have six men who work the ranch full-time, one who works part-time, one horse hand, and us." Mama Harding gestured to Haley, Silas, and herself. "We work the bed and breakfast, but it's becoming more than we can manage between the three of us. Thanks to Haley, the rooms have been full all year."

"That's great," Laney said. "I'll do whatever you need."

"I don't think we need to see a resume. A few days of having you around will tell us more about your work ethic than a piece of paper," Silas said.

"What are your living arrangements?" Mama Harding asked.

Laney picked at her fingernail. "Well, I haven't started looking for a place here yet."

"Good," Mama Harding said as if the matter was settled. "We discussed letting you stay in the cabin you were in last night. No one is using it, and it would be easier if you were closer. Town is a good twenty minutes away, and we work long hours."

Laney's eyebrows shot up. "Really?"

Mama Harding nodded. "If you're interested. The position doesn't pay much, and the cabin doesn't have TV or internet."

"I don't need those things. It's perfect."

Micah had to remind himself to breathe. Laney would be living here—in the cabin less than thirty feet from his own.

"Good," his mother said. "You can start on Monday. I was thinking Camille could go with you to town today so you could get anything you need and get used to the place. We provide three meals a day. Breakfast is at daylight, lunch is at noon, and supper is around 6:30 in the evenings. We don't have a dress code, but wear what you're comfortable in. It gets cold around here, so layers are good. Camille will know what you need."

"Camille is part of the family," Haley said. "At least she will be in a few weeks when she and Noah tie the knot."

"Okay," Laney whispered.

Mama Harding stood. "When you get back, Haley can show you about the job duties, and you can sign the paperwork."

Haley stood in a rush of excitement. "I wish I could go shopping with you. We have a few guests checking out today and some new ones coming in, so I need to get those squared away."

Laney followed everyone else to her feet. "That's great. So, I got the job?"

Micah watched as his mother opened her arms to Laney. "If you want it, the job is yours."

When Laney wrapped her arms around his mom, Micah could finally breathe. He'd be able to help her, protect her, and make sure she was happy. He had a long road ahead of him, but putting a smile on Laney's face seemed to be creeping to the top of his to-do list.

Silas reached into his back pocket and pulled out his wallet. "Here is your advance. It's for getting everything set up in your new place and any clothes you might need. We don't want you ruining your good clothes with bleach or anything."

Laney's mouth hung open as she accepted the bills. "Um. Thank you. That's very generous."

Micah had mentioned his assumptions about Laney's financial situation to his parents this morning, but he hadn't expected them to offer her anything beyond the cabin. At the sight of the money in Laney's hands, he wondered why he hadn't suggested it himself.

"Oh, and be sure to pick up an apron. It's a must if you'll be helping me out in the kitchen," Mama Harding added.

"Okay," Laney agreed. "Thank you. This is much more than I expected."

Haley stood and snapped her fingers. "We need to get some coverage on that shiner. I have a concealer that will be perfect." She rushed out of the room without an objection from anyone.

"Well, I guess that's taken care of." Micah rubbed his jaw, thankful that Haley had taken the lead on that topic and hadn't upset Laney in the process.

"I have to get back to the kitchen. The dishes don't clean themselves." His mother wrapped Laney in another gentle hug. "Welcome to the ranch, dear."

"We're glad to have you," his father added. "We can use all the helping hands we can get around here."

Laney lifted her chin with a new confidence. "I'm ready to work."

"Camille will be here in a few minutes, and Haley can get you fixed up before then." His mother waved a farewell as she stepped back into the kitchen with his dad following close behind.

Micah shoved his hands in his pockets. "So, you think you're up to this?"

"Up to it? I think I just stepped into a dream." Laney's voice was high and full of excitement. "I think I need to run a few laps around the house. My hands are shaking."

"Don't get too worked up. It's just a job, and you'll need that energy. Trust me. The ranch never sleeps."

Laney's shoulders relaxed and she gave him a grateful smile. "Thank you so much. I'm so glad my car broke down in front of your ranch."

Micah chuckled. "I wouldn't go that far. We could skip the part about running out of gas. Speaking of—"

Laney held up a silencing hand. "No need for a lecture. I know better than to let that happen again."

"Good. I don't want to think about what could've happened to you if you'd been alone."

"But I wasn't alone. You were there," she reminded him.

"Yeah." He'd be sure to thank the good Lord for that when he laid his head on the pillow tonight.

Laney eyed the bookshelf again, and Micah heard a nagging voice inside telling him to do something else for her—something simple that he could give her.

"Why don't you take one?" he said.

"Take what?" Laney asked, wide-eyed.

"A book. You don't have a TV or anything at your cabin. You'll need something to do when the sun goes down."

"Oh, no. I couldn't take any." Laney tucked her hands around her body.

"Why not? No one else is reading them. Take one and exchange it for another when you finish it."

Laney tapped her toe on the rug that spread over most of the living area.

"Come on. It won't hurt anything, and I'm telling you it's okay." He wanted to assure her without being pushy, but he was toeing the line between enough and too much.

"Okay." She ran to the bookshelf and leaned forward to read the spines.

Haley entered the room holding a small pink bag with a golden zipper. "I know it's in this bag. I just have to find it." She sat in one of the chairs and began digging through the contents.

"I need to get going. Do you need anything else? Haley will stay with you until Camille gets here."

"Oh no. I'm fine. Thank you again."

"Good." Micah nodded. "See you at lunch."

Haley waved a hand. "Oh, Camille will probably take her to lunch somewhere in town. They won't want to rush."

"Okay. See you later then." Why was he dragging his feet? He had a dozen things to do today, and he didn't have time to keep standing here.

Laney left the bookshelf and sat down beside Haley. She smiled at him, and he made himself turn and walk out.

So, Laney was staying. He wasn't sure what he should think about that yet. His thoughts were a swirl of indecision. He wanted her to stay. That was his selfish side talking. But the business-minded ranch manager side cautioned him to tread lightly. When his parents passed everything along to him, he'd be responsible for every worker on the ranch.

Even now, he felt an instinct to do right by Laney. It wasn't obligation or responsibility. It was personal, and that fact terrified him. When he started muddying the waters between personal decisions and business decisions, things could get messy.

He stepped out into the brisk morning air and donned his hat. The cloudless sky was bright, and with Laney taken care of, he needed to focus on his job duties.

They were doing the right thing giving Laney the job, and he had no doubt she would be an asset to the ranch. Haley and his mother needed the help with the bed and breakfast.

Camille parked beside his truck just as he stepped from the porch.

"Good morning!" Camille's greetings were always over the top and peppy, something Micah didn't understand.

"Morning." He pointed over his shoulder with his thumb. "We hired a new housekeeper this morning. She's waiting for you inside."

"I heard! I can't wait."

"Make sure she gets everything she needs,"

Micah said with a stern look he reserved for handling business.

Camille dismissed him with a *pfft*. "I've got this. She's in good hands."

Camille stepped past him into the house, and Micah made his way to his truck. Micah had worked the ranch since he was old enough to walk, and never once had he begrudged his duties, no matter how rough. Today, however, he felt an uneasy tugging in his chest. He set his sights on the day before him, knowing it was the first time he'd ever wished for a day off.

CHAPTER 5
LANEY

Haley pulled another tube of something from the makeup bag. "I think this one should do it."

"What is it?" Laney asked.

"Concealer. I'm sorry." Haley dropped her hands to her lap. "I should have asked you first. Do you want me to cover it up? I just assumed."

Laney held up a hand. "Of course. I didn't have anything to put on it this morning, and it was hurting so bad I didn't want to touch it."

Haley grimaced and sucked air through her teeth. "Yikes. That sounds awful. Is it okay now?"

"Much better. Micah gave me some pain relievers when he picked me up."

Haley opened the tube and squeezed a drop onto her finger. "That was nice of him. Much sweeter than the first time he met me."

Haley touched the concealer to Laney's face, and she winced. "Was he mean?"

"No. Not mean. Just a little unfriendly. He had a lot on his mind, and I took him by surprise." Haley laughed. "It's really a funny story." Her mirth intensified as she fell into a fit of giggles.

Laney couldn't help but laugh along. Haley's cackle was contagious. "Was it that funny?"

"Not at the time, but I can laugh about it now. Oh, to know then what I know now."

"I'd love to hear about it," Laney said.

"There you are." A beautiful dark-haired woman burst into the room and halted as soon as she noticed Laney. "Hey." The greeting was filled with uncertainty and pity.

"Hi. I'm Laney Parker." She stood to offer a hand. "Haley was just helping me cover up this conversation starter." She waved a hand in front of her face.

"I'm Camille. Did you put up a fight?"

The chuckle that bubbled out of Laney surprised her. "I wish I could say I did. I wasn't prepared."

Camille pursed her mouth to the side. "It won't happen again, right?"

Laney's eyes widened. "Not if I can help it."

Camille nodded once, satisfied with Laney's response. "I hear we're going shopping."

"You don't have to babysit me today. I'm sure I can find my way into town."

"Oh no. I'm so in," Camille said as she rubbed

her hands together. "Let's get your war paint on and figure out where we're going."

Laney listened as Haley and Camille threw out names of shops in town. Haley was gentle as she applied the concealer, and Laney hoped the pain reliever lasted through the shopping trip.

"What's our budget?" Camille asked.

"Um, whatever the Hardings just gave me," Laney said. "That's the only shopping fund."

Camille gave Laney a wink. "I know how to make your dollar count. How do you feel about thrift stores?"

Haley perked up. "Oh, that's a great idea." She turned to Laney. "Camille is the best at finding thrifty fashion. I have no idea how she does it."

"I work there," Camille said. "I see those clothes every day."

"You work at the thrift store?" Laney asked. Camille carried herself with an air of sophistication and confidence that Laney didn't associate with a bargain store.

"Only every other Saturday now. I just started at a law firm in town."

Laney turned to Camille as Haley reached for another tube in the bag of cosmetics. "You have two jobs?"

Camille shrugged. "When it's two jobs I love, I don't mind it. Plus, Noah has two jobs. I can't let him outwork me."

"Is Noah your husband?" Laney asked.

"Fiancé. We're getting married in a few weeks."

"Congratulations." The initial intimidation Laney felt meeting Camille had faded. She might be beautiful, but she had yet to look at Laney with an upturned nose.

"Thanks. I'll be going from being an only child to having four brothers and a sister." Camille smiled at Haley.

Laney's attention drifted back and forth between the women, and it felt as if someone had grabbed her heart and squeezed. What she wouldn't give to be adopted into a big, loving family.

But she didn't *have* anything to give. Nothing more than the clothes on her back.

"Haley!" a childlike voice yelled from a different room.

"Duty calls." Haley stood and yelled, "I'm in the den!"

A young boy burst into the room and barreled into Haley's outstretched arms. "Hay-Hay!"

"Hey, wiggle worm." Haley wrapped the little boy up and twirled in a circle. When she rested the boy back on his feet, she gestured to Laney. "This is Laney. She's going to be working at the ranch now." Haley straightened and ruffled the little boy's hair. "This is Levi. He's the boss."

Laney tried to smile, but the movement hurt her face. "Hey, Levi. It's nice to meet you."

Levi tilted his head and asked, "What happened to your face?"

She leaned down and propped her hands on her knees. "I had an accident." That was a lie. Devin hadn't accidentally hit her. "Well, I mean..."

Haley laid a hand on Levi's shoulder, and her voice was gentle yet firm as she explained, "She has a bruise. That's all you need to know."

"Does it hurt?" Levi asked.

"It does. What makes your bruises feel better when you get hurt?"

"Mama Harding puts a bag of peas on it. I can get you one! They're in the kitchen."

Laney smiled and endured the pain. "That's so sweet of you, but I'm okay. Thank you for offering."

Haley rested her hand on the boy's head. "Levi is Aaron's boy. He's around here somewhere. I expect you'll meet him at supper."

Laney added Aaron to the list of names she'd learned this morning. She hadn't known what to expect from the short job ad she'd printed at the library, but everyone she'd met at Blackwater Ranch had been kind to her so far. The least she could do was remember their names.

Camille checked her watch. "We'd better get going if we want to take our time."

They said their good-byes to Haley and Levi, and Laney followed Camille back through the house and out the front door.

"Mine is the 4Runner." Camille gestured to a vehicle parked on the left side of the porch.

Laney settled into the passenger seat and marveled at the interior of the new car. "Wow. This thing has more buttons than an airplane."

Not that she would know what the inside of an airplane looked like, but she'd seen them in movies where pilots sat in front of a huge panel of lights and switches.

"It's pretty new. I had a wreck last year, and I needed something better suited to the snowy roads around here."

A sting of panic poked Laney in the chest. Her tiny car might not hold up to snowy roads. There hadn't been a need to drive much in Cheyenne. She lived close to the bar where she worked. Devin had rarely allowed her to venture out, and she'd given up asking a long time ago.

"How many people work here?" Laney asked.

Camille backed up to turn the car around. "Let's see. There's Silas and Anita."

"I met them this morning."

"Then their five sons."

Laney whistled. "Five. And they all work here?"

"Yep. They live in the wranglers' cabins. Noah and I are building a house on the ranch that's big enough for a family, and Asher and Haley are probably about to start on their home too."

Laney squashed the pang of jealousy that bubbled up in her middle.

"Then there's Maddie," Camille continued. "She mostly keeps to the stables with the horses."

"Is that Levi's mom?"

"Oh no." Camille shook her head. "His mom isn't around. She died a few years ago, but she'd left the ranch well before that."

Laney gasped. "I'm sorry. I didn't know."

"She wasn't happy, and she had an addiction problem. I wasn't around when she was still here, but I'm sure the Hardings tried to help her. Levi doesn't ask about her much. Probably because we keep him busy."

Laney's thoughts swirled in confusion. The little boy had seemed so happy. There hadn't been a trace of sadness this morning.

Camille reached over and patted Laney's hand. "Hey. I didn't mean to upset you. We all love Levi so much, and we make sure he's taken care of."

"It sure seems like he's okay." Laney had grown up with both of her parents, but they'd barely paid attention to her. Yet, it was a balm to her wounded heart to know that Levi was happier with one parent than she'd been with two.

"He's a handful," Camille said with a smile. "I can't wait to have more kids around here."

"Is someone expecting?"

"Not yet. But Asher and Haley just got married,

and Noah and I would like to start a family soon after we're married. We both want kids." Camille's shoulders crept up in her excitement.

Laney wasn't sure how to process the enormity of the love these people shared. Newlyweds, kids, families, and friends—the ranch was full of it.

She hung her head and twisted her fingers around a knuckle. She'd only known a life of angry words and reprimands. It felt as if she'd stepped into a different world where kindness covered everything, making colors brighter and hearts warmer.

The Hardings were the family she'd gone to sleep wishing for as a child. In her adult life, they'd been the family she'd longed for but had lost faith in its existence.

Maybe if she hid her brokenness well enough, they'd let her stay.

Laney lifted her head, determined to prove her worth to these people. If she worked hard enough and did whatever they wanted, she might have a chance of keeping this job.

If there was one thing she'd learned from working for Devin, it was that she could be a good machine. Turn on, do your job, shut down, repeat.

Camille turned into a parking lot beside a building. A large Blackwater Restoration sign lined the top, and windows lined the front of the store.

When she shifted into park, Camille turned to Laney with a sweet smile. "Listen, I don't know your story or how you got roughed up, but I'm letting you know now that you can talk to me in confidence."

Laney breathed deep. Why did it feel as if she'd been holding her breath? "Thanks. I'm just going through a rough patch right now."

That was a lie. Why did she keep spitting out untruths?

"I mean, I think I'm on the other side of a rough patch that has been my life. Despite the bruises, this is the most hopeful I think I've ever felt."

Camille gave a single nod. "Good. The past doesn't matter. I don't care how many times you've fallen. Get up, get up, get up, buttercup!"

And with her motivational speech completed, Camille stepped out of the vehicle, spurring Laney into action.

"Try this one." Camille piled another shirt onto Laney's outstretched arms.

"These look brand new." She touched the hem of the blouse Camille had just found in the sea of clothing at Blackwater Restoration.

"You just need to know where to look. Go try those on, and I'll meet you in the fitting room."

Laney carried the mound of shirts, jeans, and jackets to the back of the store and locked herself in an empty changing stall. She caught sight of her reflection in the full-length mirror and turned away.

She didn't want to look at herself until the bruise was gone.

Anger boiled within her. How could Devin have done this to her? She'd worked herself into the ground for him, and all he'd given her was a broken face. She shouldn't have trusted him, but his honey-laced words had lured her in.

She held up the first shirt. It was a stylish navy sweater with a V-neck. She checked the tag out of habit and gaped at the cheap price. Camille certainly had a gift for finding treasures.

The soft material slid over Laney's skin as she tugged it down over her middle. The fit was perfect, and she turned to the mirror.

Yep, that ugly bruise was still there, but the sweater was soft and warm, and she didn't mind so much that her face was busted up.

"Laney," Camille called from the other side of the door.

"Coming." Laney stepped into the hallway where Camille waited with more clothes.

"I love that one! Put it in the keep pile."

Laney smiled, but the expression turned into a grimace.

"Here." Camille put the clothes on an empty chair and dug into her purse. "You need some medicine."

Laney sighed. They'd been shopping for hours now, and the task had kept her mind off the pain most of the time. "Thank you. Micah gave me something this morning, but it's wearing off." She took the offered pills and dry-swallowed them.

Camille stepped into the dressing room and grabbed the pile of clothing they intended to purchase. "We need to wrap this up soon. You'll need food in your stomach now."

Laney turned to the mirror at the end of the hallway between two rows of fitting rooms. The sweater was beautiful, and she couldn't wait to wear it again.

There was a sticker at the top of the mirror, and she stepped closer to read it.

Today is never too late to start over.

Laney wrapped her arms around her middle and hoped the words were true. Today certainly felt like the start of something new.

"Okay, leave the others there, and I'll go through them tomorrow." Camille gestured to a red basket at the fitting room entrance. "Micah just texted me and asked if I had fed you yet, and I don't want to respond until I can say yes. The boss means business."

Camille disappeared back into the store, and Laney stood paralyzed. Micah was checking on her, and she wasn't sure what to make of the warm fuzzy feeling swirling inside of her. All she knew was that it made her suck in deep breaths to keep the moisture from pooling in her eyes.

Laney gave the sticker one last glance and stepped back into the fitting room to change out of the sweater and back into her own clothes. As she slid the lock into place, she knew today was a new beginning.

CHAPTER 6
MICAH

Micah stopped at the edge of the porch and kicked his steel-toe boots against the side of the main house, dislodging dirty snow and mud. He was early for supper, and he dared anyone to call him out on it. He was usually the last one in, but today he had a bone to pick with Camille. She hadn't texted him back. Did she think he didn't want an answer after he took the time to send her a text? Why did she have a phone if she wasn't going to use it?

He stepped onto the porch at the main house and toed off his boots. Inside, he hung his hat near the door and ruffled his hair. He'd never cared much about how he looked, but today he wished that hat hair wasn't a thing.

The meeting room was empty, but he knew

Camille had to be around here somewhere. Her SUV was parked out front.

Micah stuck his head into the kitchen where his mother was pulling cornbread out of the oven. "Hey, have you seen Camille?"

His mother wiped her hands on a dish towel. "She's upstairs with Haley and Laney."

"What are they doing?" he asked.

"Haley was going over the job duties with Laney, and Camille tagged along."

Micah breathed a sigh of relief. If the women had been together all day, someone would have called him if Laney needed him.

As if she needed him. He'd been hovering over her since she'd arrived, but she hadn't once asked for anything. Just because she was appreciative of over-the-counter pain relievers and a book to read didn't mean she needed him.

"Thanks." He slipped back out of the kitchen and up the stairs. They only had two rooms filled right now, so it was the perfect time for Laney to get into the swing of things without being overwhelmed. The bed and breakfast had really taken off in the last few months thanks to Haley and her online marketing. She'd somehow turned a working ranch with a few spare bedrooms into a bustling vacation destination.

He'd been skeptical about the changes to the ranch, but his mother was a hostess at heart. She loved having people fill her home, and Haley had stepped into a managerial role with ease at the beginning of the year.

Feminine laughter filled the upstairs hallway, and Micah followed the bubbly sound. The door to the last bedroom on the right was open, and he peeked in to find the three women sitting on the bed.

Haley waved her hands in the air as she tried to contain her laughter. "So, I said, 'I'll catch you in the morning,' and he was like, 'Nah, I'm leaving before breakfast. Have a nice life.'"

Camille brushed a tear away from her eye as she sucked in deep breaths followed by more laughter. "He's so dense."

Laney covered her cheeks and laughed. The sight of her covered in happiness was shockingly beautiful. Camille and Haley joked around and laughed all the time, and he hadn't thought twice about it. But when Laney laughed, he felt drawn to her like a magnet. He wanted to give in and let the force snap them together.

"Hey, you." Haley's greeting snapped him out of his daydream of sealing his lips against Laney's smile.

Micah propped his shoulder against the doorframe, pretending he didn't feel like a bungee strap, pulled taut and ready to snap. "I'm not dense. I'm focused."

The women jerked their attention to him, and Laney straightened. The laughter drained from her in an instant.

Geez, he thought they were kidding around.

"You totally blew Haley off!" Camille reminded him.

Micah crossed his arms over his chest. "And everything turned out just fine."

"That's the truth," Haley agreed. She turned to Micah and lifted her hands, palms up. "Sorry, but you're not my type."

"Agreed. What are you ladies up to?"

Camille stood and straightened the bed covers. "We were just giving Laney the tour. She's going to be starting Monday morning."

Laney stood and straightened her shirt. "I can start tomorrow."

Haley waved a hand, dismissing the offer. "Tomorrow is Sunday. We only do the minimum on the Lord's day."

Laney tilted her head slightly as if confused.

Micah studied her as the women moved toward the door. He stepped aside to allow Camille and Haley to exit, but Laney hung back just inside the doorway. She rubbed her knuckle for a second before shoving her hands into the back pockets of her jeans.

"Hey." Her soft voice was unsteady and nervous.

"Hey," Micah echoed. "How was your day?" The

question was broad, but he'd asked exactly what he wanted to know. The hours since her interview this morning felt oddly blank, and he wished she'd fill them in with detailed descriptions of the things he'd missed.

Laney shrugged. "It was great. Haley helped me cover up my face, and only a few people stared."

The thought of strangers giving Laney questioning glances or making her feel uncomfortable didn't sit well with him. "Did you have lunch with Camille?"

Laney's shy smile tugged at the corners of her mouth. "We went to Sticky Sweets Bakery. I met your brother, Noah. He stopped by."

"Good." Micah rubbed the back of his neck. "I should have sent more medicine with you this morning."

Laney's shy smile grew wider. "Camille gave me something. I really appreciate everything you've done for me."

He wasn't sure what to do with her gratitude. Every move he made from sun up to sun down had a purpose—an objective to move the ranch forward—but the things he wanted to do for Laney fell outside of that category. He swallowed hard and tried not to think about how absent-minded he'd been all day worrying over her.

"You're welcome." He pointed a thumb toward

the stairs leading down into the meeting room. "It's almost suppertime. You hungry?"

"I could eat." Laney stepped through the doorway, only inches from him, and her sweet smell filled his senses.

"What did you think of Sticky Sweets?" He fell into step beside her, uncharacteristically happy merely because she was in better spirits than she'd been yesterday or this morning.

"It was delicious. I had a cream cheese filled puff pastry that I'll be dreaming about for weeks."

They reached the stairs, and Micah gestured for her to lead.

Laney stood at the top of the stairs, looking down into the meeting room. Mingled voices drifted up to them, but Laney didn't move.

"Is everything okay?" he asked. A cord of tension tightened in his spine as he waited for her to respond.

"Oh, yeah. I'm just nervous about meeting everyone. I know I've met a handful of them already, but there are a lot of people here."

Micah inched closer and brushed his pinky finger against hers. "Hey, they're all nice. No one is going to bother you here." He glanced down the stairs. "You'll probably meet my cousin, Hunter. He looks intimidating, but he keeps to himself. He never bothers anyone."

Laney kept her gaze focused on the room below. "Got it. I can do this."

Before he could agree with her, she gently wrapped her pinky finger around his.

Roaring filled his ears until the voices downstairs faded away. He hadn't realized he was drowning until he took this first breath. How could the smallest touch evoke such a powerful reaction?

His gaze met hers, and he stilled, holding the breath that had brought him to life.

"Can I sit by you at supper?" Laney whispered.

His reaction was delayed. He'd been overwhelmed by the force known as Laney Parker. "Of course." The words sounded even and assuring. Exactly what he'd hoped would come out of his mouth while he tried to settle back down from cloud nine.

With his assurance, she released his finger and took the first step leading to the meeting room.

Throughout supper, she stayed close to his side, and he introduced her to everyone. After meeting a few of his brothers, she seemed to relax, though she remained beside him as if they were connected by an invisible rope.

What could have happened to her that caused her to be wary of meeting her new coworkers? He hadn't doubted everyone would welcome her to the ranch. With the bruise almost covered, no one asked about it or even gave it a second glance.

When supper was over, she was diligent in saying her farewells, showing thanks and pleasant grins for everyone.

Micah didn't rush her. He stayed close enough that she could easily find him when she was ready to leave. He watched as his mother wrapped Laney in a hug. She seemed like a different person from the woman he'd met yesterday. That person had been tired and sullen, but not a trace of her weariness remained. Seeing her smile reaffirmed his decision to open the vacant cabin to her and offer her the job.

Laney scanned the room, and Micah raised his hand to get her attention. When she spotted him, she made her way over. Her chin was lifted, and her shoulders were pushed back, full of confidence and poise.

"I didn't mean to make you wait," she said.

"No problem. I'm not in a hurry." Micah grabbed his coat off the rack and turned to her. "Do you have a coat?"

"No. I left mine at the cabin after we finished shopping today."

"Here. Take mine." He handed her the heavy coat. "It'll be big, but it'll do its job until we can get you in for the night."

Laney took the coat from him, and he didn't move until she'd slipped her arms into the sleeves and folded the front over each side of her small frame.

"You ready?" he asked.

"Ready and warm."

Satisfied that she wouldn't be shivering, he opened the door and gestured for her to go first. He opened the passenger door of his truck for her and waited until she was settled in before he took his place in the driver's seat.

"So, what do you think about the job?" he asked as the engine roared to life.

"It was great. This is definitely the best job I've ever had, and I haven't even worked my first day."

"Where did you work before?" he asked. She'd mentioned a bar, but not much else.

She focused on her hands resting in her lap. "I worked at a few restaurants before I worked at Dive In. It's a bar just outside of Cheyenne." She lifted her chin. "It wasn't a great place to be, but it was something. I don't have any experience in housekeeping."

Micah didn't like the idea of Laney working in a bar at all. He gripped the steering wheel and pushed the thought from his mind. "That's not a problem. Mama and Haley will help you get into the swing of things. They'll need someone to greet incoming guests and clean the rooms when someone checks out. They'll need help with laundry and cooking too."

"That's what Haley told me. I'm sure I can handle that. I'll just help out wherever I'm needed."

Micah appreciated her attitude about the new

job. He'd had the same job since he was old enough to work, but that didn't mean he didn't have to learn new things. Laney seemed to welcome the challenge.

He parked the truck in front of her cabin and got out. She'd slipped from the truck before he could meet her at her side.

"I'll install a motion sensor light on the cabin. It comes in handy when you get in after dark."

"Thanks. I didn't realize how dark it would be. I can't see a thing."

Micah offered her his hand to guide her to the porch steps, and she took it. The feel of her hand in his had his chest swelling with pride, and the contact warmed him more than any coat. "Three steps."

When they reached the door, he scratched the stubble on his jaw. "We don't have locks on these cabins, but I can get you one if you want."

Laney took a deep breath and hesitated. "It's fine. I don't expect anyone to break and enter here, right?"

"That hasn't happened here before."

"I don't need it then. Plus, you're right next door."

Warmth spread in his chest knowing she was confident he'd protect her if she needed him. "Right."

She opened the door and peeked in. When she

found the light switch, she flipped it and opened the door wide.

"You want me to start your fire?" he asked.

"Please. I'll watch you so I can learn how to do it myself next time."

He admired her initiative every time she insisted on learning and making her own way, but it also meant that she would need him around less. Would she have a desire to be with him if she no longer needed his help?

He picked up the last few logs in the box beside the fireplace and propped them into a configuration. "You want some ventilation under the logs. These kindling bundles are the easiest way to get things going." He grabbed a few straw bundles and shoved them beneath the logs.

Laney leaned over his shoulder as he knelt in front of the fireplace. She'd stayed by his side most of the evening. Did it mean anything that she was comfortable being so close to him?

Micah grabbed the long-reach lighter and lit it. A small flame burned at the end that he stuck into the heart of the kindling. "That's the basics. You might need to light it in a few places to get things started, but just make sure it's hot enough to catch the bigger logs."

Laney stood to her full height. "I think I can handle that. If I have any problems, I know who to call."

Micah rose to his feet, far too close to Laney for his comfort, but she didn't retreat. Instead, she smiled up at him as if he were the hero who had saved the day.

No, he was imagining every scenario he wished were true. He wasn't a hero, and Laney didn't need saving.

Micah glanced at the door. "I have something for you. I'll be right back."

He strode out into the cold night and fumbled in the center console of his truck until he found the bottle of pain medicine. He raced back to the porch where she waited, bundled in his coat.

"Here. You'll need these tonight and tomorrow."

She took the bottle and examined it. "Thank you. I hope it'll ease up soon, but I may need some help getting to sleep and getting up in the morning."

Micah shoved his cold hands into his pockets. "Speaking of tomorrow morning, do you want to ride to church with me?"

Laney tilted her head and then lowered her attention to the floor. "Um, sure. What time should I be ready?"

"We'll need to leave around 10:30, but breakfast is at 7:30. I'll need to take care of a few things around here after breakfast, but I can give you a ride back to your cabin after that."

"Okay. What do I need to wear?" she asked as she pulled the coat tighter around her middle.

He needed to hurry this up so she could get inside and get warm. "Whatever you want. There isn't a dress code or anything."

Her shoulders relaxed. "Okay. Thanks." Her eyebrows rose quickly, and she sucked in the cold air. "Oh, here's your coat back. Thanks for letting me borrow it." She slid the coat off her arms and handed it back to him.

"No problem. I'll pick you up a little after 7:00 in the morning. You have my number if you need anything," he reminded her, silently hoping she'd use it for more casual purposes.

"I do. Good night. And thanks for the fire too."

Micah tipped his hat and slowly turned, reluctant to leave. Nothing had ever felt more important than running the ranch, but his attention had been divided today.

He heard the door creak closed and latch as his boot hit the last step on the porch. He'd never been so invested in anyone before. He'd always assumed that if he kept the ranch running and profitable that his family would have everything they needed. His job was to provide, and he'd never wavered from that duty before now.

He settled into the quiet cab of his truck and tossed the coat into the passenger seat. His instinct to provide now warred with the urge to help Laney.

As he shifted into reverse, he reminded himself that his only job was to manage the ranch. He'd done his part to make sure Laney had what she needed. He'd provided shelter, a job, and temporary relief from the pain someone else had inflicted on her.

With Laney squared away, he needed to focus back on his job—the one that never changed and wouldn't ever change. He was the first son, and he'd inherit Blackwater Ranch when his parents passed on. It was the future he'd always known to expect.

He turned his truck toward the shed behind the main house. Spring was coming, and that meant calving season was near and hay season wasn't far behind. The work hours were longer, and the ranch required every second of his extra time.

He parked his truck by the shed but didn't get out just yet. The urge to find a woman to love and spend his life with had been strong the last few years. Panic had set in a few times when he thought about how few women he'd ever had the chance to meet.

As he thought of Laney, he wondered if there was a chance she could be the one he'd been praying for. The fact that she was employed by the ranch didn't bother him, but she might not feel the same way. Lucas and Maddie worked together, and they had a better relationship because of it.

Any woman Micah married would need to accept the ranch as part of their life together. The idea of living and working alongside his wife had always appealed to him. His parents had been a model for the relationship he hoped to have one day.

He huffed and rubbed his hands over his face. He needed to get his thoughts in order. Laney wasn't looking for a relationship. She'd just been abused by a man, and she was skittish around everyone.

Except him.

No, he didn't need to have false hope. Laney wasn't available. She needed space and help getting back on her feet, not a boyfriend.

Resigned to put Laney out of his mind, he opened the door into the cold Wyoming night. Before he'd reached the shed, a bright light shone through the open back door of the main house.

Camille stepped out and shut the door behind her before slinging a coat over her shoulders. She tucked her hands around her body. "Hey, I hoped I would catch you here."

Micah tilted his head toward the shed. "What do you need?"

"I wanted to talk about Laney," Camille whispered.

He didn't like the uncertainty hidden in Camille's words. He tilted his head toward the shed. "Let's get inside."

When he shut the door against the cold, Camille pulled gloves from her pocket and slipped them on. "How is Laney?"

Micah flipped the light switch and shrugged.

The topic of conversation made him nervous, and he turned his attention to the firewood he'd come for. "As good as can be expected, I guess."

Camille tilted her head. "I'm worried about her. Has she told you anything about herself?"

Micah stacked firewood into his arms. Laney hadn't said much, but he also hadn't pressured her. Still, he wondered if Laney had been tight-lipped around Camille today and why. "Probably not anything more than she told you."

Actually, he was in the same boat as Camille. He wished he knew more, but he wasn't inclined to ask.

Camille stepped up beside him and began piling logs into her arms. "Do you think she's running?"

The air in Micah's lungs turned to stone. Why was it so hard to breathe when he worried about Laney? "Do you think someone might be coming for her?"

Camille didn't look at him as she picked up another log. "I've seen it before. And Laney kept looking over her shoulder while we shopped today. She's scared, and I can see why." Camille gestured to her face, indicating Laney's bruise. "But what is she scared of now?"

Micah turned to take the wood to his truck. He needed a minute to think about what Camille had said. Was someone looking for Laney? Was she leading trouble to their door? It was his job to protect the ranch, but it had somehow become his job to protect Laney too. He'd made promises to her —not in so many words, but he didn't want to break any trust she had in him. She didn't seem to have anyone else to count on.

Camille joined him at the truck and placed the firewood in her arms on top of a stack. "I want to help her, but I don't know how. When people come to me, it's because they already know they want help. I've never been in this position before, but I know the look of a woman on the run."

Camille was an attorney, and she'd changed her specialty from corporate law to family law when she moved back to Blackwater. He knew little about what Camille did, but it was apparent that she was passionate about her work. Helping people came as easily to Camille as breathing. And if Laney needed help, Camille would be the first one he'd call.

Micah scratched his cheek and leaned against the truck. "Do you think I shouldn't have hired her?"

Camille shook her head. "I think you did the right thing. She's ours now, but I want to help her. I just think she'll need to trust us first."

Micah propped his hands on the bed of the truck. "I'm not any good at this."

Camille chuckled. "I know. That's why I wanted to talk to you. I can tell you're trying, and I think you're doing a great job. She stays by your side, and that's a big start. If a man that she was once close to did that to her, it's monumental that she's allowing another man beside her. It has to mean that she thinks you're worth trusting. Someone who would keep her safe instead of hurt her."

Micah tried not to read too much into those words, but they settled into his skin and warmed his insides, despite the frigid weather. "Do you think we can help her?"

Camille smiled and patted his shoulder. "I know we can. I just wanted to tell you to keep doing what you're doing. I know this is new for you. Just keep talking to her and assuring her we're here to help. She'll let us know what she needs in her own time."

Time. What if they didn't have time? What if Laney didn't trust them soon enough, and they all got caught up in Laney's fight unprepared?

Micah closed the tailgate on the truck, and the metallic bang pierced the quiet night. "I'll talk to her."

"Good. I'm not sure I need to mention this because you've been doing a great job with her so far, but maybe tone down your... gruffness."

He huffed at Camille's low blow. "I'm not gruff."

Camille rolled her eyes. "Not really, but you're a little bit too direct sometimes, and that can come off as uncaring."

Was that really what people thought of him? He did care. He just didn't feel the need to pad his words and actions with unnecessary fluff. "I don't mean to be that way."

"I know, and everyone here loves you just the way you are. It's just that Laney is new, and she doesn't know any of us well. Your directness might make her pull away."

Micah tensed his jaw. Scaring Laney away was the last thing he wanted to do. They needed her here, and he didn't want her thinking he was a heartless manager. "Got it. I can be on my best behavior."

Camille smiled and patted his arm. "I know you can do it. I saw the worry in your eyes at supper. I've never seen you look at anyone like that before."

He wasn't sure what to say, so he kept quiet. No one had ever occupied as much of his headspace as Laney Parker.

"Good night. See you in the morning." Camille tucked her coat around her and left him alone with his thoughts.

Taking care of the ranch had always been the most important thing in his life, and it still was. But Laney was a part of that circle of his protection now, and he found himself questioning his role as a leader.

He got back into his truck and headed home, determined to be patient while Laney settled into the cabin next to his and her new role at the ranch.

CHAPTER 7
LANEY

Laney sat on the step of the small cabin porch and rustled Dixie's fur. "You can come over every morning. I don't mind."

Dixie panted and leaned into the attention. The white of her fur was a shade darker than the thin layer of snow that dusted the ground.

"I haven't ever had a dog. Not that you're mine, but I think I would have liked having a pet. People talk to pets, and it isn't weird." Laney sighed and her breath released in a puff of fog. "I never had anyone to talk to."

She looked out to the reaching acres of the ranch. The main house sat proud and lit by the sun peeking over the tree line. "I love sunrises. They remind me of beginnings." Laney looked at Dixie and smiled. The bruising hurt more than yesterday, despite the medicine Micah had given her. But the dog always looked like she was smiling, and it made Laney want to do it too. "Is it okay to hope this is a new beginning?"

Dixie nestled her big body under Laney's arm and plopped down in her lap.

"I'll take that as a yes." She hugged the dog tighter to her. She rarely saw the sunrise. She'd worked later hours at Dive In, and the day really started when the sun went down. Sunset meant it was time to plaster on a smile and sidestep grabby hands. Sunset was a warning to keep her eyes and ears open and her head down. She was only meant to be seen and not heard.

But when Dixie looked up at her with those wide eyes and bright smile, it made Laney think her new friend liked it when she talked.

When Micah brought her home last night, she'd found the dozens of voicemails and messages from Devin waiting for her. Since she was using the phone as her alarm, she'd woken up to the same barrage of notifications this morning. The mere sight of them had started her morning off on the wrong foot.

As if she needed more to compound her anxiety, she'd tortured herself by listening to the voicemails. Each was as nasty and malicious as the last. He'd used words she'd heard him save for his worst enemies. His voice had haunted her dreams, banging on the walls of her mind and piercing her heart like knives.

By the end of the string of threats, she'd been sick to her stomach and wondering if leaving had caused more harm than good.

No, she was much better off here at Blackwater Ranch snuggled up to Dixie who seemed to be picking up on her sinking mood.

"I'm okay, girl. Just a little worried." How long was Laney going to keep lying? She was more than worried, and *okay* was certainly an overstatement.

The only truth was that she was trying—trying to hope that this was really the fresh start she'd always hoped she'd get. The Hardings hadn't judged her, and they hadn't held it against her that she'd been a man's punching bag.

She'd wandered around the quiet cabin this morning, unsure of what to do. She hadn't ever lived alone, and the unencumbered space felt like a trick. Someone would walk in any moment now and crowd her into a corner, reminding her that she was to be quietly pushed aside. She wanted to welcome the silence and wallow in it like fresh snow, but she was afraid to accept it—the freedom she desperately craved. Everything could change, and if she welcomed the peace, it would break her heart to give it up.

Laney shook her head and tightened her hold on

Dixie. "I'm sorry. You shouldn't have to put up with my pitiful mood."

She closed her eyes and remembered the words she'd read on the sign in the dressing room yesterday. "Today is never too late to start over." She opened her eyes and massaged Dixie's ears. "You think that's true?"

Dixie barked, and Laney laughed. The dog's perfect timing almost sounded like a response, and tears pooled in Laney's eyes. "You're right, sweet girl. I think it could be true. At least that's what I'm going to believe today."

A banging startled her, and she and Dixie both turned toward the sound.

It was Micah closing the door of his cabin beside hers. He shoved his feet into his boots and set his hat atop his head. He hadn't looked her way yet, and she took the opportunity to watch him. He stood tall with his shoulders squared as he stepped off the porch and walked through the crunchy snow toward her.

When he noticed Laney and Dixie on the porch steps, his relaxed expression turned up in a smile that had hope building in her middle. How could she be anything but happy when that kind smile greeted her at the start of every day.

"Morning." His voice was hoarse, as if those were the first words he'd spoken since waking up.

"Good morning," she replied. Those simple

words from Micah topped the list of beautiful greetings she'd never known existed.

"How are you feeling?"

The kindness in his question struck her in the chest. The best greeting she'd ever gotten from Devin was "Get up," and the worst was too horrible to repeat.

Laney stood and Dixie trotted over to share her own greeting with Micah. "I'm okay." It didn't feel like a lie anymore, and she felt relieved. She only wanted to tell Micah truths. She wanted to trust him, and she wanted to give him the same.

Micah stood beside the porch and offered a hand to Laney. "Let's go get some breakfast."

She hesitated to grab his hand, unsure of what he was doing. There were three small steps from the porch to the ground. Was he really offering a helping hand to take three steps?

Before she'd recovered from her confusion, Micah shoved the hand in his coat pocket.

Great, she'd waited too long, and he'd taken the offering back. He'd misunderstood her hesitation. She wanted to take his hand, but no one had ever been so chivalrous to her before. Heat filled her cold cheeks and tingled her ears as she tucked her hands in the pockets of the new coat she'd bought yesterday and followed Micah to his truck.

He opened the passenger door for her before walking around the front to the other side. Once they were settled inside the cab, he started the truck and made a three-point turn. He looked over his shoulder and then at the path leading to the main house, but never at her. She suddenly didn't like the silence and wrapped her coat tighter around her body. Devin had always yelled when he was mad, but maybe Micah was the type to torture with silence.

When they parked at the main house, Laney opened the door and jumped out. When she closed the door, she realized Micah had rounded the truck. Her shoulders hunched forward, and she feared the unknown more than the devil she knew.

"Are you all right?" Micah asked.

"Yes." Her word was clipped, and the lie tasted like mud in her mouth.

"Are you sure?" he asked. "We can slip into the living room and talk if you want. Do you need some more of Haley's makeup? Did the medicine not work this morning?"

"No. Well, I would like some makeup, but I can't keep using her stuff. I know makeup can get expensive. The medicine worked fine this morning. It's just hurting a little more today."

Micah rubbed the back of his neck. "Listen, we can eat breakfast in the kitchen again if you want. Or you can make a plate and take it back to your cabin. Breakfast isn't a meeting that requires attendance."

Maybe he wasn't upset with her. His questions

about her wellbeing were thoughtful as always. "I'm sorry about not taking your hand back there." She flippantly waved her hand toward the row of wranglers' cabins. "I just got nervous."

Micah hung his head. "It's okay. I was a little too forward, and I sometimes forget what you just went through."

"It's not that. I... I like that you offered. It was very nice. It's just not what I'm used to."

"What do you mean?" Micah asked with a furrowed brow.

She waved her hand again as she tried to think of the right words. "It's very sweet. I don't think a man has ever opened a door for me or offered me a hand to walk down stairs."

Micah's grin tugged to one side. "I've always opened doors and done things like that."

Laney tucked her chin in embarrassment. He was doing all of those sweet things for her out of obligation. It was ingrained in him as much as any other habit.

"But I want to do those things for you. I know it's old-fashioned, and you can open the door for yourself. But if it's okay with you, I'd like to keep doing it."

Laney nodded. "Okay." Talking to Micah was a million times easier than talking to anyone she'd ever met before. Camille and Haley were creeping up to tie for second place.

Micah gestured toward the door. "Let's get inside where it's warm. We need to find Haley before everyone gets here."

She followed him up the steps and to the door where he removed his boots. The warmth of the meeting room hit her face and thawed her insides. She'd been sitting on the porch with Dixie just to have someone to talk to. The one-sided conversation was worth the bone-chilling cold.

They found Haley in the kitchen, and she greeted them with a cheerful "Good morning." Her auburn hair was tied up in a high ponytail that whipped from side to side.

"Oh! I need to get you that makeup. I'll be right back."

Before Laney could respond, Haley was darting from the kitchen.

Mama Harding turned from the oven carrying a tray of biscuits with mitts. "Good morning. How are you feeling this morning, Laney?"

"I'm okay. Is there anything I can help you with?"

Mama Harding pointed toward a large bowl. "Can you put the biscuits in that? Micah, will you get the jellies?"

He nodded and did as his mother asked. Laney followed suit, and they fell into a series of tasks to prepare the breakfast for the ranch workers and guests.

Haley burst back into the kitchen and beckoned Laney to follow her to the den. They sat facing each other on the couch as Haley applied the cosmetics that would hide the worst of the bruise. The swelling was the same as yesterday, but that couldn't be masked.

Haley gently rubbed her fingertips over the bruised area. "I'll put these in a bag for you and leave it by the door. You can keep them. I never use these."

"You don't have to do that," Laney whispered.

"I really don't mind. They're not doing me any good. I wear so little makeup these days."

The two fell into a comfortable silence until Haley leaned back to observe her work. "There. You can barely tell."

"Thank you," Laney said as she stood.

Haley threw the last of the compacts into her bag. "Let's get to breakfast. I'm starving."

The meeting room was bustling now, and Laney hung back away from the crowd. She didn't want to mess up any of the names she'd learned last night, so she quizzed herself to match the name to each face. Everyone moved in the room like bees in a hive.

She spotted Micah at the end of the serving counter and found her place at his side. Mama Harding announced that breakfast was ready, and that each person could serve themselves from the buffet-style serving counter, reminding everyone that guests could make their way to the front of the line.

A few couples that Haley had introduced Laney to the night before shuffled to the serving counter. They chatted with one of Micah's brothers that Laney thought was Lucas. After filling their plates, they chose a small table set for two near the far window.

As the Hardings made their way through the line, they took their plates to the long table that ran the length of the room. Just like the evening before, Silas was last through the line and remained standing after he laid his plate of food on the table.

She knew what was coming—the prayer—and it reminded her of Micah's invitation to ride with him to church today. She bowed her head like everyone else as Silas said his thanks for the food, the family, and the guests.

Laney didn't know much about prayers, so she stayed quiet and listened.

"And today we are thankful that You sent Laney to us. I pray that she finds peace and healing at this table, and You cover her with comfort."

At the mention of her name, she held her breath and every muscle in her body tensed. Being called out by name made her self-conscious. She didn't want any extra attention. She wanted to keep her head down and earn her place here. Why was Silas thankful for her? She hadn't even put in a day's work at the ranch yet.

When Silas finished the prayer, everyone lifted their heads and picked up their forks. No one spared a glance for her. Maybe he hadn't drawn attention to her after all.

The prayer only reminded her that she had no idea what to expect at church today. Could she make an excuse to get out of it? Being in a new place was hard enough, and she didn't want to think about all the curious looks she'd get from the nicely dressed people. What would she wear? Maybe the new sweater she'd bought with Camille at the thrift store.

Everyone talked throughout breakfast. When their plates were empty, they sat and talked about the few things that needed to be done before church. Micah ticked off tasks, and a few of his brothers volunteered to take care of them.

Once the meeting room was cleared, Micah appeared at her side.

"Are you ready? I can take you back to your cabin until it's time to leave for church."

"Sure." She followed him out and into his truck.

Neither of them spoke, but the silence didn't feel uncomfortable. She got the impression that Micah was thinking about the work he'd just been assigned.

He stopped in front of her cabin and shifted into

park. "Do you want me to get your fire going again?" he asked.

"I don't think so. I kept it going last night, and it was fine when I left this morning."

Micah looked impressed when his eyebrows raised the smallest fraction. "Okay. I'll be back soon. Call me if you need anything."

"I will. Thanks."

She jumped from the truck, and Micah drove off to take care of the morning jobs. Dixie met Laney at the porch, and she stopped to pet the friendly dog.

"Did you miss me?" Laney asked.

Dixie barked once before stilling at Laney's neck scratches.

"I missed you too." She breathed in the fresh, cold air. "Do you know anything about church?"

Dixie didn't reply, but Laney sat on the top step of the porch and got comfortable.

"I don't know anything about church or God. What am I supposed to do?"

The dog settled her head into Laney's lap as she continued to scratch her ears.

"I guess I'll just keep my head down and figure it out as I go." It was what she always did, and it had gotten her through so far.

CHAPTER 8
MICAH

Over the last few days, Laney had fallen into her new position at the ranch, and Micah watched her grow comfortable in the main house. Every morning, she waited for him to pick her up on the small porch of her cabin. Dixie was always at her side, as if Laney had turned the working dog into a lap dog.

Guests checked in and out of the bed and breakfast, and Laney made them feel welcome. With her shoulders pushed back and her chin high, she looked as if she had always been an ambassador for the ranch.

Laney worked quickly and thoroughly, if Haley's praises held any merit. It seemed Laney was a natural hostess.

Micah kept his attention on her for many reasons, but he tried telling himself that his interest in her was merely business. After her first week of work, her drive and willingness to help wherever she could had thoroughly impressed him, as well as the other Hardings.

Each night after supper, she stuck around to help clean up the meeting room with Mama Harding. Micah usually tended to a few more things around the ranch before coming back to pick her up and take her to her cabin. They'd fallen into a routine, and he liked knowing what to expect. He offered to build her fire in the evenings just to have an excuse to spend a few moments alone with her. He slept better at night knowing her cabin was warm.

The next weekend was busy. Everyone was scrambling to get ready for spring and the extra work that came with the longer hours. On Saturday evening, Micah barely kept his head up during supper, and every other worker wore similar worn-out expressions.

Laney seemed to be working double time. She cleared the empty plates from the tables while the other workers stumbled through the end of the workday meeting.

When the last of his brothers had dragged his feet out the door, Micah sought out Laney. She wiped the serving counter and barely looked up at his approach.

"I have a few more things I need to do before I

call it a day. I can take you home before I get back to work."

Laney shook her head. "I have a few loads of laundry to finish up, and I haven't put away the dishes. Would you mind coming back by when you're finished?"

"Sure, but you don't have to work so late. That stuff can wait till morning."

She shook her head. "I'd rather do it tonight."

"It's okay to take a break," Micah reminded her.

She leaned her hip against the serving counter and brushed a hair that had fallen out of her pony-tail to rest behind her ear. "This is my job now. I want to be helpful."

"And you have. I promise you, we're all thankful you're here. But I don't want you working yourself into the ground."

Laney crossed her arms over her chest. "Says the man who is about to go put in hours ten through thirteen." She raised her brows, daring him to disprove her.

Micah grinned. "You got me there, but I love my job. Keeping this place running is important."

"And I think I'll do the same."

Micah reached for her hand, and she allowed him to hold it, dropping the other to her side in surrender.

"You're worth more than the work you do here. I

know better than anyone that a job can overtake everything in your life if you let it."

Her gaze fell from his face to his chest, as she processed his words. He knew little about her life before she came here, but anyone could see that she was used to working long hours.

He brushed his thumb back and forth over her hand and wondered if he would ever stop worrying about her. He didn't understand why it was so important to him to know that she was content here, but after a week of Laney taking up most of his headspace, he doubted it would change anytime soon.

Micah was used to working his days away, but lately, he'd wished for more hours outside of the demands of the ranch. If things didn't change soon, he'd live his entire life working for the land, and for what? So he could have the privilege of dying here? He wouldn't have anything to show for those back-breaking work days. What was he working for if he didn't have a loving wife to go home to at night? What would all of this matter if he didn't have a family to benefit from his work when he was gone?

For the first time he realized that he wanted more than the ranch. He wanted someone to share his life with and a family to love. Having Laney here made him wish for more with her, opening his eyes to a new world he'd never thought about before she came along.

He cleared his throat and asked, "Did you pick out a book?"

Her grin widened. She smiled much easier now that the swelling in her cheek had gone down. "I haven't yet. I've been going to bed early. I'm not used to working the daylight hours yet."

"Call me when you're ready for me to take you home, or you can pick out a book and hang out in the living room until I get back."

She squeezed his hand and let hers fall from his gentle grasp. "I think I'll do that."

"Okay. I'll be back soon." He turned away before the urge to stay here with her all evening became too enticing. If he could get his chores done quickly, he could get her back to her cabin by 9:30.

Micah didn't waste time as he worked his way through his list. He could focus on the work if getting done early meant seeing Laney sooner. Spending time with her was the best motivator, and he accomplished three hours of work in a little over two.

The lights at the main house were dimmed when he returned. Only one light was still on in the meeting room, and he walked through the house looking for Laney.

He stopped short when he made it to the living room. Laney lay on her back on the couch. Her eyes were closed, and she looked peaceful with a blanket draped over her legs and a book open on her chest.

The TV was on, but the sound was turned down low. The lights were off, but a reading lamp glowed above her head.

Micah smiled at the sight of her sleeping soundly. He'd done it. He'd made her feel comfortable and safe long enough to stop looking over her shoulder and relax.

He quietly moved closer and leaned over where she slept. The Holy Bible laid open with her hands still holding each side.

He recalled watching her through the church service last weekend. It had been too late when he'd realized he'd mistakenly assumed she was a believer, or at least one who went to church, so he'd snagged one of the gift Bibles from the vestibule and handed it to her before they entered the sanctuary. She'd sat between him and Camille during the service, and he'd helped her find the passages as they were mentioned. It hadn't occurred to him that she might not regularly attend church until he'd seen her discomfort through the service. She'd squirmed the entire time, and her eyes had darted all around the room watching everyone else.

Since then, she'd bowed her head during each mealtime prayer without hesitation, but he hadn't yet figured out how to ask her about her faith. She seemed accepting, but he didn't know the condition of her relationship with the Lord.

Seeing her now, sleeping with the Bible in her

hands, gave him hope. If she was seeking the Lord's word, she was at least moving in the right direction. Wasn't that what they were all trying to do, move closer to Christ?

He sat in the recliner next to the couch and rested his head back. Sinking into a comfortable chair when his bones were tired was the best feeling. Knowing Laney was safe and close-by only made it better.

CHAPTER 9
LANEY

Laney stretched her arms above her head, and a loud thump jarred her quickly from sleep. Her heart raced as she sat straight up, prepared to face the cause of the noise.

She was in the living room of the main house, and Micah was rubbing a fist over his eyes in a nearby recliner. On the floor beside the couch lay the Bible she'd been reading.

Laney willed her breathing to slow. The thump must have been the book hitting the floor. She propped her elbows on her knees and rubbed the heels of her hands in her eyes. The bruised cheek protested on her right side.

Micah groaned and stretched his arms out to his sides. His wide chest and muscular arms strained against the charcoal thermal shirt he'd worn yesterday.

So much for settling her heart rate. The sight of the handsome man five feet away had her adrenaline running wild. What a way to wake up.

Micah squeezed his eyes closed and sat up in the chair. "Morning."

"Good morning." She covered her cheeks with her hands, certain they were turning red to mix with the yellowish tint of the healing bruise.

"How did you sleep?" he asked in a husky morning voice.

What a casual question. She'd been jolted out of a deep sleep to instant embarrassment. Her ponytail was probably a bushy mess.

How had she slept? Beautifully, until the end. "Fine. I can't believe I fell asleep here. What time is it?"

Micah reached for his phone on the end table and looked at the screen. "Just after 6:00."

"I'm so sorry." She stood and picked up the Bible.

Micah sat forward. "It's not a problem. You looked comfortable when I found you. I couldn't wake you up."

She tilted her head slightly. "Did you sleep here because I fell asleep?"

He stood and stretched his arms above his head. Was she going to get distracted every time he flexed those muscles?

"Well, I didn't want you to wake up and not have a ride back to your cabin."

Her cabin. Would she ever get used to that? It wasn't truly hers, but she liked to entertain the idea of making it into a home of her own. She'd never had her own place, and doing domestic things like decorating sounded like way too much fun.

"That's so sweet of you. I hate that you slept in that uncomfortable chair."

Micah looked at the recliner behind him. "I didn't notice. I fell asleep before my butt hit the seat."

Laney chuckled and covered her mouth with the back of her hand.

He stepped closer to her, and all smiles were gone. This man did strange and wonderful things to her insides. She could even smell him when he was this close. How did he smell so good first thing in the morning? It wasn't a clean smell. More like a strong man smell. Wood and pine.

Laney set the Bible on the end table and reached for the remote to turn the TV off. "I can't believe I left the TV on too."

Micah scratched his face. "It's probably the most use it's had in the last ten years."

Laney had fallen asleep quickly to the sound of the characters talking on the television. The voices had made her feel as if she wasn't alone, and it was the best sleep she'd had in a while. She looked back to Micah. Maybe she'd slept so well because she *hadn't* been alone.

Micah tilted his head toward the door. "Let's get you home. We can both get cleaned up before breakfast."

"Of course." Laney led the way back through the main house, hoping no one saw her wearing the same clothes she'd worn yesterday.

They were both quiet on the ride to the cabins, and Laney brushed a hand over her matted ponytail. Micah had already seen her at her worst, but it still bothered her that he was seeing her tangled hair.

Micah parked his truck in between their two cabins. He turned to her and brushed a hand over his own hair and asked, "Do I have bed head?"

Laney tilted her head and squinted one eye. "I think it looks good on you."

Micah raised his eyebrows, and she wondered if she'd gone too far. It was hard to ignore her attraction to him. It was like walking around an elephant in the room.

But when Micah looked at her with that easy grin, she couldn't regret her words. Maybe there was a playful side beneath the all-work-no-play exterior.

"I'll meet you back here in thirty minutes."

Laney opened the door and jumped from the high truck seat. "Thanks for the ride and for hanging around last night." She looked at her shoes, unsure of what else to say. It was incredibly sweet that he hadn't left her alone.

Micah tipped his hat to her. "It was my pleasure."

Laney turned to hide the blush creeping up her cheeks and ran to her cabin. Inside the silence greeted her again. She'd never been much of a television watcher, but she suddenly wished for the convenience of background noise. Maybe she should get a radio.

She tiptoed into the quiet cabin and found her phone on the nightstand by her bed. Her heart sank at the number of messages. Devin hadn't stopped texting her since she left. The number of notifications was outrageous.

Laney tossed the phone back onto the bed and turned to grab a clean outfit. She'd seen enough from that quick peek at her phone to know that some of the messages contained threats. What could he possibly want with her? She'd been hoping for a clean break, but it seemed Devin wasn't giving up.

She sucked in a deep breath and puffed it out quickly. At least he didn't know where she was, and he had no way of finding her here. She hadn't even told him which way she would be going.

She bundled the clothes to her chest and stood. She spared one last glance at the phone on the bed.

Why did she even keep it if the only person who called her was Devin? She had been using her phone as an alarm in the mornings, but she could run into town and get a cheap alarm clock.

Laney forced her worries about Devin out of her mind as she showered. He wasn't here, and she didn't want him to ruin her day. She tied her long hair into a wet bun and checked the bruise. It looked better than last week, but it was still colorful.

She had just finished applying the concealer Haley had given her when she heard a knock at the door. She practically skipped through the cabin, ready to see Micah again after only half an hour apart.

Laney threw open the door to find Maddie on her porch instead. Her blonde hair was neatly plaited and fell over one shoulder.

"Morning, sunshine. Micah had to run out early this morning, and he asked me to pick you up."

Laney had met Maddie a few times now, but they hadn't had a chance to talk much yet. She knew Maddie was engaged to Micah's brother, Lucas, and they both cared for the horses on the ranch.

"You didn't have to do that. I can drive my own car," Laney said.

Maddie waved her hand in the air and tsked behind her teeth. "It's no problem. I'm on my way to breakfast anyway."

Laney grabbed her coat off the rack by the door.

"In that case, I'll take you up on that offer." She followed Maddie to a pickup truck and slid inside.

Maddie shifted into reverse and looked over her shoulder. "How are you liking it here so far?"

Laney twisted her finger in her lap. "I love it here." Her voice lowered to a whisper. "I really want to fit in."

Maddie nodded as she watched the path ahead. "I know what you mean. I came here less than a year ago, and I remember hoping and praying I would fit in." Maddie's smile grew as if she were replaying a favorite memory. "The Hardings make it easy. They took me in without hesitating. I was the one who was reluctant to believe I could have a chance here." She turned to Laney with a knowing smile. "I was wrong, and I'm glad."

"I would never have guessed you had only been here for less than a year. You seem like part of the family."

Maddie shrugged. "I *am* part of the family. Lucas and I aren't married yet, but they've been the family I never had."

Laney looked at the various trucks parked in front of the main house. "They sure are special."

Maddie shifted the truck into park and killed the engine. "You said it, sister. The only thing you have to do around here is be yourself. The rest will fall into place."

Laney got out of the truck and hoped Maddie was

right. The problem was that Laney didn't know who she really was. Every move she made had been dictated by Devin for years now. He told her when to get up, what to wear, when to work, how to work, and where and when she was allowed to go anywhere.

Having a work schedule now was comforting to her, but she didn't know what to do in the hours in between. Thankfully, the bed and breakfast kept her busy. There was always something to be done around the main house.

A high-pitched squeal greeted them at the door. "Maddie! Laney!"

Levi got a running start and barreled into Maddie's arms.

"Morning, sunshine," Maddie said as she squeezed the boy tight before resting him back on his feet.

Laney was next, and she opened her arms to the little boy's bubbly greeting. "Hey, buddy."

He wrapped his arms around her neck and squeezed tight. Levi had warmed up to her as quickly as everyone else, and his bright personality always put her in a good mood.

"Can I sit by you today?" Levi asked Laney.

"Of course. I'd love that." Laney ruffled his hair.

Levi ran off to join the others while Maddie and Laney got in line to wash up.

Micah still hadn't shown up when Mama

Harding called for everyone to line up. It looked like they would be eating without him.

The question of Micah's presence swirled in her mind throughout the meal, but no one seemed to be concerned. Did he often work through meals?

After breakfast, Maddie gave Laney a ride back to her cabin, and they went their separate ways to get ready for church. This would be Laney's second week attending church, and she hoped she would feel more comfortable this time. She had gone in blind before, but it had been a great learning experience.

In the last week, she'd gotten a chance to read the Bible Micah had given her. Unfortunately, it had only raised more questions. Maybe if she continued to listen in church, she would learn the things she needed to know.

A few hours later, Noah and Camille showed up at Laney's door. Noah was one of Micah's quietest brothers, and Laney found him easy to be around. He never expected her to explain herself, and he didn't ask too many questions.

Noah gestured to his truck. "Micah is running behind this morning. You want to ride to church with us?"

"Sure. Thank you so much. I could drive myself, but I don't really know the way yet."

Camille slipped her arm through Laney's.

"There's no need to drive yourself when we have room."

On the drive to church, Laney asked Noah a few questions about his job as a firefighter. It was hard for Laney to understand how he could work two demanding jobs. After hearing him talk about his passion for the work he did, she understood why he made great sacrifices to do his best for both positions.

Camille laid a gentle hand on Noah's arm. She looked at her fiancé as if he were her hero. "I'm always impressed when he works a long shift for the fire station and comes home to pick up work at the ranch.

"When you love your job, it doesn't seem like work," Noah said.

Laney looked at Camille and asked, "What about you? You have two jobs, don't you?"

Camille nodded. "I do, but I may have to give up my position at the thrift store soon. I can still volunteer there, but there are a lot of clients counting on me to do my best for them."

"What's it like being an attorney?" Laney asked.

Camille grinned. "It's all I've ever known. I love it, and I love helping people."

Laney wondered if Camille dealt with situations like the one she was having with Devin right now. Did Laney need to get a restraining order against Devin, or would that only lead him to her door?

It didn't matter; she didn't have the money to pay for legal help. And really, Devin hadn't done anything but fill up her phone with calls and texts since she'd left. That wasn't really hurting anyone, was it?

She didn't want to think about him this morning. She wanted to enjoy the church service and the feeling of peace she'd felt last week when she'd attended. She wanted more of that in her life—the good times when she felt safe and surrounded by people who cared about her.

Laney stayed close to Camille as they entered the building. Camille stopped and spoke to everyone she passed, introducing Laney as the newest member of the ranch's team.

Levi grabbed Laney's hand and guided her to sit beside him. On her other side sat Camille. The pew was overflowing with the Hardings by the time a skinny older man with glasses stepped up to the podium. She relaxed into the cushioned seat as she looked from one side to the other. She was covered on all sides by good people. A warm feeling of peace washed over her, and she turned her attention to the speaker.

Everyone settled into their seats, and the mumblings of the crowd died to a whisper. Just as the man at the front greeted everyone, a loud click drew her attention to the back of the room. She turned to see Micah slowly walking up the center aisle. He wore a crisp plaid shirt and dark-wash jeans with clean boots.

She released a heavy breath and felt the last piece of the puzzle fall into place. Micah was here, and she had everything she could ever want right here beside her.

With her worries gone, she was able to focus on the preacher. He spoke of the power of faith and the promises found in God's word that His children should look to Him for guidance.

His words rang with power and truth, and each time she began to question the enormity of His promises, the preacher read the words from the Bible in front of him. At first, Laney scrambled to find the parts he read from in the book, but she gave up and decided to listen instead. She'd have to learn how to find things in this big book, but that would come in time.

The preacher's booming voice filled the large room. "We were never promised that life would be all roses, but He is with us every step of the way. You show me your mountain, and I'll show you my God. Show me the depths of your sorrow, and I'll show you the comfort of my God. Show me your remorse, and I'll show you a God of forgiveness."

Laney's breath jerked to a halt at his words, and she felt as if someone had kicked her in the chest. His confidence was so strong in his God that she wondered how she could ever question His power.

Her chest swelled and filled with a different kind of air. It felt like the first real breath she'd taken in her entire life.

She'd heard of God and church, but she hadn't really known anything. How had she gone her whole life without knowing about the Bible and the power of God?

Suddenly, she was back in school. Every word the preacher spoke seeped into her skin and settled in her blood, coursing through her body and sinking into her soul.

She thought about Maddie's advice from earlier. She could be herself here. They had taken her in when she needed them most, and now they'd introduced her to a church where she was learning about the hope that could be found in the Bible Micah had given her.

When the service was over, she felt three inches taller. The Hardings side-stepped out of the pew to where Micah waited for her with an easy smile on his face.

"Sorry I wasn't around this morning. We had a truck breakdown, and it took me a while to get it back up and running."

Laney stood next to him as the churchgoers shoved them closer to each other. "It's okay." She wanted to tell him how she'd missed him, but she let her smile say it instead.

Micah leaned down closer to her and lowered his voice. "Want to ride home with me?"

That was one offer she was happy to accept. The first time he'd welcomed her to his home, he'd changed the course of her life. Now she knew that home with Micah was her favorite place in the world.

CHAPTER 10
MICAH

Micah rushed to take his boots off at the door of the main house. He was almost late for lunch. He'd gotten tied up at Grady's Feed & Seed when they'd mixed up his order for a new feed bin, and it had taken half an hour on the phone with the supplier to get the order fixed.

There was already a line at the serving counter with the Kepharts leading the way. The spunky elderly couple had been guests at the bed and breakfast for almost two weeks now, and Micah was beginning to wonder if they were ever planning to go home. They always sat at the main table with the family, and they had become fast friends with everyone.

Micah spotted Laney hanging back by the washroom and set his course straight for her. It had been two weeks since she showed up at the ranch, and she had rarely left his thoughts. Having Laney at the main house gave him a sense of peace wrapped in urgency. He liked the thought of her being close, but he also didn't like leaving her between meals.

Laney's smile grew when she spotted him. That smile did crazy things to his stomach, making it feel like he was falling from a high cliff.

He darted into the washroom and quickly lathered up his greasy hands. His mother would never approve of the quick wash, but she'd have to forgive him this once.

Back in the meeting room, he spotted Laney in the same place as before and stepped up beside her. His fingers tingled, aching to touch her, but he fisted them at his sides.

"Hey. How is your day going?" She was probably getting tired of answering the same question every time she saw him, but he couldn't resist asking.

"Great! The Kepharts just extended their stay, and we have two new guests checking in after lunch."

Micah didn't care so much about the guest list, but Laney was always excited to welcome new people. It made her happy, and that was all that mattered to him.

He gently brushed his fingertips over the bruise on her cheek. "This is almost gone."

She turned to him and her gaze met his. He was acutely aware of how close he was standing to her, but he couldn't force his feet to back up. If he leaned down just a few inches...

Whoa. Hold your horses. Micah mentally reined himself in. Laney wanted a job and a place to stay, not kisses and longing stares.

"I hardly notice it anymore."

The remaining bruising could be completely covered by the makeup she'd gotten from Haley, and while he wanted to believe Laney was fully healed, he knew some injuries held on for the full eight seconds, no matter what you did to shake them.

Micah cleared his throat and scanned the food line. "Where is Jameson? He was here this morning." Jameson worked the ranch part-time, but he'd assured them he could put in some extra time this week.

Laney shrugged. "He hasn't shown up yet. Should someone call him?"

"Nah. He knows when to come in for lunch." Micah just hoped Jameson hadn't been called away to one of his other jobs. They had a lot going on this week to prepare for the calving, and he needed every hand he could get.

"Let's get in line." Micah gestured for Laney to step ahead of him, but she didn't move. Her eyes were wide and locked on something behind him.

Micah looked over his shoulder to see Jameson making his way across the meeting room. When he turned his attention back to Laney, a shocked stare greeted him.

"Laney? What's wrong?" He gripped her arm as her expression turned into one of fear.

Why would she be afraid of Jameson? Sure, the man was a few inches taller than Micah, but he wasn't intimidating or harsh.

When Laney didn't speak, he turned back to Jameson and noticed his leg. The jeans on his right leg were dark from the knee down.

Laney whispered, "Is that... blood?"

Micah turned back to her, but her stare was turned down toward Jameson's leg.

"Laney?"

Micah had barely gotten the word out before her eyes drifted closed and her whole body began to lean toward him. When she fell against him, he wrapped his arms around her to keep her upright. "Laney!"

She sagged in his arms, and he adjusted his hold to cradle her.

Jameson knelt beside him. "What happened?"

"Is that blood?" Micah asked, tilting his head toward Jameson's leg.

"I cut it on the edge of the feeder in the north barn. It's not bad, but it bled for a little bit."

Micah held out a hand to halt the crowd of people rushing to their side. "Let's get her out of here, and you can check her out." Jameson was a paramedic in the same firefighter crew as Micah's brothers, Noah and Lucas. Micah's pulse raced as he carried her into the living room.

He gently laid her on the couch and knelt beside her. "Laney. Laney, can you hear me?"

Jameson lifted her legs and shoved a couch pillow beneath them. "I'll get her some water."

Micah picked up Laney's hand and held it tight between both of his. "Laney. Come on. Please wake up." He wanted to believe she'd fainted at the sight of the blood, but what if something worse was happening?

He reached to grab his phone from his pocket to tell Jameson to bring the medical bag. Before he could make the call, Laney made a small grunting sound.

"Laney." Micah cupped the uninjured side of her face. Her skin was softer than he'd imagined, and he moved his hand around to cradle the back of her neck. "Laney, are you okay?"

She blinked a few times, but it looked as if she wasn't truly seeing him. He held his breath as he waited for her to speak.

She looked around the room before her gaze landed on him. "What happened?"

Jameson entered the room, and Micah whirled around to meet him.

"Whoa. Give me that." Micah took the glass of water from Jameson and pointed back the way he'd come. "You can't be in here right now in case she fainted because of the blood. Send Noah and Camille."

Jameson turned on his heel and hobbled back through the door.

Micah resumed his place at Laney's side. "Don't get up. You fainted. Are you feeling okay? Did you eat today?" He tried to remember how much of her breakfast she'd eaten, but he was having trouble thinking straight.

"I'm okay." Laney groaned and held a hand to her head. "Was he bleeding?"

"Yeah. He said he cut his leg. I'm sure he's fine or he would have said something. Do you always faint when you see blood?"

"Not always, but that was a lot of blood. It just —" She leaned up to prop on her elbows.

"Easy now. Don't sit up too fast."

Laney squeezed her eyes closed. "I won't fight you on that. I'm still fuzzy."

Noah and Camille entered the room, and Camille rushed to Laney's side.

"Hey, you gave us quite a scare. What's wrong?"

Micah stood to give Camille room, though he still wanted to be close to Laney. He crossed his arms over his chest next to Noah. "It looks like Laney can't handle the sight of blood."

"Reactions like fainting happen to some people,"

Noah said. "It was probably just a vasovagal response."

"Does she need to see a doctor?" Micah asked.

"No!" Laney answered from where she lay on the couch. "I mean, I'm really okay."

He wasn't sure what to make of Laney's response to his suggestion that she be evaluated. He turned to Noah, hoping to hear the same response from his brother. If Noah thought she would be okay without seeing a doctor, Micah would trust his brother's word and feel much better about all of this.

Noah nodded. "She didn't hit her head, or injure anything in the fall, so I think she'll be fine with just some rest."

Micah turned back to Laney in time to see her relieved expression. What aversion did she have to doctors, and did it have something to do with her issue with blood? "I'll get her home, and she can take the rest of the day off. We'll see how she feels after that."

Camille handed Laney the glass of water, and she sat up to take a slow drink. "I really think I'm okay. I just need a minute to let the dizziness go away."

"No way," Micah said. "I want you to take the rest of the day off and stay off your feet. We can manage around here for half a day."

Laney's brows pulled together, and she shifted her gaze to the floor.

Micah knelt beside her again. "It's really okay. I would rather know you're fully recovered before you get back to work."

"Okay." Laney's acceptance was soft and reluctant.

Micah turned back to Noah and Camille. "I think she's okay. I'll let her rest here a little longer and then take her back to her cabin."

Camille patted Laney's leg. "Call me if you need anything."

Laney smiled weakly. "Thanks. I'm sorry I caused such a big stir over nothing."

Camille tilted her head and grinned. "We care about you. Just focus on feeling better."

"Okay. I'll see you later." Laney waved her good-byes to the couple as they left the room.

Micah didn't move from where he knelt beside her. He wanted to hold her hand again, but he wasn't as eager to make that move now that she was conscious. He'd been so worried when she fainted that he'd forgotten to give her space.

His feelings for Laney were growing quickly. They were spreading like a wildfire, hot and uncontrollable. But she might not feel the same for him. All the more reason he should give her the space she needed. He didn't want her to feel forced into anything.

But he couldn't control his feelings for her. When she'd collapsed into his arms, panic had over-ruled everything. It was his worst fear—that he would lose her before he even had a chance to tell her how he felt. He'd been trying to make sense of the emotions she stirred within him for weeks, but it didn't change the fact that he didn't know how to balance a relationship and his job with the ranch. It was all new to him, and he owed it to her to get his act together before he pledged a commitment to her.

If she even wanted a relationship with him.

Laney turned her head on the couch pillow and looked at him. "I'm so embarrassed."

Micah chuckled. "No reason to be embarrassed. Things happen."

"Speaking of things happening. How often do people get hurt like that around here?"

Micah scratched his jaw. "Scratches and bruises are common, but major injuries happen maybe twice a year. Once if we're lucky."

Laney rolled her head back. "Oh boy, this isn't going to be fun."

He couldn't resist the urge any longer. He gently lifted her hand in his and brushed his thumb over her skin. "Now that we know you don't get along with blood, we can be careful to make sure we don't come around with our cuts."

Laney huffed. "I think I'm ready to get up."

"You sure? You can stay here as long as you need."

"No, I'm really okay." She gripped his hand and pulled herself up to a sitting position. "Yeah, I'm fine now."

"Stand up slowly," Micah said.

Laney pushed to her feet, and Micah kept his hands on her arms in case she decided to topple again. What he wouldn't give to be this close to her when she didn't need him to keep her standing.

"I'm okay," she whispered.

That was his cue. He should back up and let her go, but he wanted to stay close to her. He wanted her, and the craving consumed his every thought.

It took every ounce of fortitude to move away from her. "I'll pull the truck around back so we can sneak out that way. I doubt you want to face everyone's questions."

"Right. I'd rather sneak out."

He stalked back through the kitchen and meeting room, letting everyone know in as few words as possible that Laney was okay and he was taking her home to rest. He quickly made a plate for her and covered it with foil in the kitchen. Then he pulled his truck around the house and parked it at the back door. Back inside, Laney was studying the bookshelf.

"Do you want to take one with you?" he asked.

She reached for a thin book on the lower shelf. "I

think I'll take this one." She tucked it under her arm and met him at the door.

When they were settled inside the truck, Micah asked, "Are you sure you're feeling okay?"

"I'm sure. Thank you for helping me." She turned to him and narrowed her eyes. "Did I fall?" She rubbed a hand over the back of her head.

"No. I caught you before you got that far."

Laney tucked her shoulders in and wrapped her arms around her middle. "You did? Thank you. I'm glad you were standing so close."

He was glad he'd been standing so close too, for more than one reason. "Me too. Why didn't you want to go to the doctor? I could have taken you."

Laney shook her head. "I don't have health insurance, and I can't afford a bill like that."

Micah gripped the steering wheel. "Laney, don't worry about it. Your insurance is right here." He pointed at his chest. "I'm not going to let you sit around not getting help when you need it. I'll cover anything like that."

Laney sat up straighter. "No, you won't. Do you know how much something like that could cost?"

"I do, and I stand by what I said." He wasn't budging on this topic. "Don't ever think I would let you go without something like that. I'll talk to Dad and figure out how to get you on the ranch policy."

"No, please," Laney pleaded. "You've done so much for me already. I can't ask for insurance too.

I'm really fine. I rarely have to go to the doctor for anything."

Micah rested his hand on hers. "Laney, I'll take care of it. It's nothing to worry about. You're a full-time employee, and you qualify for the insurance plan."

"Micah—"

"It's happening. Stop worrying about it," Micah said.

Seconds of silence ticked by before Laney laid her other hand atop his. "I can't thank you enough for all you and your family have done for me."

"Don't mention it. We're happy to do it." He said the words with ease, but a nagging thought pierced his good mood. If he told her how he felt about her, would she go along with him because she felt as if she owed him something? Surely she knew he wouldn't turn his back on her if she turned him down. He would never fire her or deny her anything if she decided she didn't feel the same way about him as he did about her.

But how could she know? She didn't know him well enough, and it sickened him to think she would assume.

What did he do now? Should he continue to give her little hints about his growing feelings for her? Did he back off and let her come to him in her own time? But what if she was too cautious to do that?

He parked in front of her cabin and ran around

the front of the truck to help her out. She might still be dizzy, and he didn't want her falling out of his high truck.

He grabbed the plate of food and stopped at the door as she went inside. "I'll bring your coat and a plate of food for supper. I need to get to the north barn and see what kind of mess Jameson made."

Laney twisted her finger. "I'm really fine." She took one step closer to him and laid a hand on his arm.

His adrenaline was firing on all cylinders, and his heart beat loudly in his ears. Every muscle in his body screamed to lean in and kiss her.

She took the plate from his hands, and her voice was soft as she said, "Thank you for everything."

Micah could barely hear her over the roaring in his ears. What was he supposed to say? He couldn't think of the words right now. Instead, his gaze darted from her eyes to her lips and back. How did this woman take away his ability to think straight?

He cleared his throat and looked away from her to get his head on straight. "You're welcome."

"I'll see you later?" she asked with a lilt at the end.

"Yes, ma'am," Micah promised.

She closed the door, and he walked back to his truck, mentally kicking himself for clamming up. When he parked on the other end of the ranch, he looked back the way he'd come. The cabins were too far away to see, but he still felt that invisible tug toward Laney.

He rubbed both hands over his face, unsure why he couldn't think of anything but her. Sure, she was beautiful, but she was kind and appreciative and determined. Her drive alone made her irresistible. Watching her getting more comfortable in the main house every day was like watching a balloon fill with air. Laney stood straighter and stronger each day.

Micah knew his feelings for Laney would only grow, and leaving her alone didn't feel like an option. Until she told him to hit the road, his only choice was to continue to let her know he cared about her and hope that one day things between them could grow into something more.

CHAPTER 11
LANEY

"Shh. You have to be quiet or you'll get us caught." Laney pressed a finger to her lips.

Dixie wove around the broom as Laney tried to sweep the floor.

"Stop it," Laney giggled at the attention-seeking dog. "How am I supposed to sweep if you keep walking through my pile?"

She continued chuckling and half-heartedly shooing the dog out of the way with the broom she'd named Roger. She'd found the broom in the coat closet, and she'd been using it every day. How did the cabin floor get so dirty when she spent hardly any time here?

Someone knocked on the door, and Laney covered her mouth to restrain the yelp.

Laney turned to Dixie and put her finger up to

her lips again before whispering, "Go, hide in the bedroom."

Dixie pranced off in the direction Laney had pointed, and she breathed a sigh of relief when the dog was out of sight. Wishing she had x-ray vision or at least a peephole, Laney rested her ear against the cold wooden door.

"Who is it?" She felt ridiculous hiding a dog in her bedroom, but she hoped whoever was knocking wouldn't stay long and Dixie could come back out to play.

A deep voice answered, "It's me." After a pause, he amended, "I mean, it's Micah."

Laney threw open the door with a welcoming smile. "Hey."

He held up a white bag in one hand and a plate wrapped in foil in the other. "I'm delivering dinner."

As if summoned by the food, Dixie came trotting around the corner.

Laney put her hands on her hips. "Dixie! I told you to lay low."

Dixie barked in response, and Laney laughed.

"I thought I heard you talking to someone in here," Micah said.

"I hope you don't mind. I really wanted some company."

Micah shrugged. "It's fine with me. Dixie is spoiled as it is. She'll be expecting to sleep at your feet every night."

Laney turned to the dog and tilted her head. "Well, I wouldn't mind that so much myself. I think Dixie just found herself a bed buddy." She waved Micah into the cabin. "Get in here. It's freezing."

"I wouldn't call this freezing."

Laney closed the door behind him. "I'm always cold. I swear I was made for the tropics. Too bad I've never been out of Wyoming." She picked up the broom and stored it back in the closet on her way to the kitchen. "Thank you for bringing dinner. I hadn't really thought about food yet. I was sweeping, and Dixie was keeping me busy."

Micah moved into the kitchen and put the plate and bag on the table. "We've had Dixie for a few years now, and she's a good one. She's like an extra hand when it comes time to move the herd."

"I never had a dog growing up, and it's nice knowing that either you or Dixie are always close by."

She immediately felt ridiculous for admitting that she liked having him near, and she hurried to turn the conversation. "Do you want something to drink?" she asked.

"I'm okay."

"You sure? I can make us a pot of coffee." She tried not to sound desperate, but she'd been in this cabin alone for hours, and she wanted him to stay.

Micah pulled out a chair at the small table in the center of the kitchen. "I guess I could use a cup."

She started making the coffee. "What have you been doing all day?"

Micah rested his arms on the table. "Fixing equipment mostly. We need everything up and running for the busy season. We have a short summer, and we have to make every minute count. A lot can go wrong quick if we have to stop everything to fix the machines."

"Sounds like a hard day. You make me feel bad for lying around all day."

Micah chuckled. "Don't worry about it. What about you? What have you been up to?"

She leaned her back against the counter and crossed her arms over her chest. "Well, I unpacked all of my clothes."

"You hadn't done that yet?" Micah asked.

"No, I wanted to make sure I was staying first."

Micah's head jerked up. "You were planning to leave?"

"Oh no. I just didn't know if I would get the job or if you'd decide to cut me loose because I was a lousy worker or something. I've been around the block enough to know that not every job works out."

"Okay. Well, I certainly think your job is safe."

"Good. Then, I built the fire, cleaned the bathroom, and read some in the devotional I borrowed from the main house."

"You like it?" Micah asked.

Laney tucked her chin and said, "I do. It's

helping me understand what I read in the Bible. I don't know if I told you, but I haven't been to church before."

"I assumed. I'm sorry I didn't figure that out sooner. I could have at least told you what to expect."

The coffee pot sputtered, and the smell of brewing coffee relaxed her. "It's okay. I'm getting used to it now. I'm just starting at square one, and it's a little overwhelming."

Micah rose from the table and joined her beside the coffee pot. Every nerve ending sent jolts of electricity through her body, and she sucked in a deep breath to steady the onslaught.

He stopped only inches in front of her, and the smell of wood mixed with motor oil filled her senses.

"I'm sorry I didn't talk to you about it." His voice was deep but soft enough to wash over her sensitive skin, pebbling gooseflesh on her arms.

"It's no big deal," she whispered. They were so close, it felt unnecessary to speak at a normal volume. Embarrassment heated her face, and she suddenly felt weak as water. "I'm sorry about today." Nervousness took over her words, and she regretted bringing up the incident when it had been forgotten.

"I'm glad you're okay. You had me worried."

Laney wanted to lean into him. She wanted him

to wrap her in his strong arms and hold her. No one had ever worried about her before. Not her parents, not her roommates, and certainly not Devin.

"I didn't mean to worry you."

Micah raised a hand and brushed the back of his fingers along her bruised cheek and down her jaw. She held her breath and relished the comforting touch.

"I always worry about you," Micah whispered.

The beep of the coffee pot jerked her out of the trance Micah had put her in. "I'll get us some cups." She stepped away from him and sucked in a breath as she grabbed for two mismatched mugs and filled them with coffee.

They sat at the table, and she unwrapped the plate. "This smells delicious."

"Mama is the best cook," Micah said.

"She sure is. Maybe I can learn a thing or two from her. What are you up to for the rest of the evening?" Laney asked before shoving the first bite of meatloaf into her mouth. It was delicious, and she stifled a contented groan.

Micah leaned back in his chair. "I have some office work to do tonight, so I'm heading back to the main house when I leave here."

"What kind of office work?" she asked.

"Paying bills, ordering supplies, checking the local ranching forums. I put off the business side of things until it piles up. Can you tell it isn't my favorite part of managing the ranch?"

Laney dug into the thickened potatoes. "That's what I used to do for the bar. I paid bills and kept up the inventory during the day and worked behind the bar at night."

Micah yawned and grabbed his cup of coffee. "I'm going to need this if I'm going to make it through the evening."

"Do you ever slow down?" she asked.

He shook his head. "Not really. The ranch has a lot of moving parts, but I'm responsible for all of it."

Laney pushed the food around on her plate. "You don't have to sit here with me if you have something you need to take care of."

Micah leaned forward and rested his arms on the table. Dirt and grease stained his hands and disappeared beneath his coat sleeve. "No, I'd much rather be here."

Laney's heart flooded. It meant a lot to her that he gave her his attention when he was being pulled in multiple directions. It showed he cared enough to put everything aside for her.

"What's in the bag?" she asked.

Micah slid it to her. "Dessert."

Laney narrowed her eyes at him as she opened the bag. She pulled out a thick puff pastry from Sticky Sweets Bakery. She'd tried one on her shopping trip with Camille and mentioned to him that it was delicious.

Tears welled in her eyes before she'd even processed the gift. She couldn't even afford a specialty cup of coffee, and he went out of his way to not only make sure she had everything she needed, but he selflessly gave her something she wanted.

She blinked hard to disperse the tears and lifted her head to Micah with a tight grin. "Thank you." If she said any more, her voice would shake, and she would let the tears of gratefulness fall.

She hummed in satisfaction as she chewed the first bite.

Micah chuckled. "Is it that good?"

"Here. Try it." She offered the delicate pastry to him, and instead of taking it from her, he leaned in and took a bite.

He chewed slowly, rolling the flaky goodness around in his mouth before saying, "You're right. It's delicious."

They could be a cute couple in a cheesy romantic movie right now. Drinking coffee and feeding each other puff pastries. The scene was so comfortable that she wanted to plant herself right here with Micah Harding and grow roots.

She lifted the dessert to her lips and paused to ask, "Tell me something about you."

Micah scratched his cheek and studied the wall

behind her. "Well, I guess Haley told you I'm color blind."

"Oh, yeah. She told me how the two of you met. I can't believe she mistook Asher for you. The two of you are as different as night and day."

"Truer words were never spoken. Asher is great, and he's a hard worker, but getting him to take anything seriously is like pulling teeth."

Laney chuckled. "You seem more like your brother, Aaron."

"Yeah. We're a lot alike. He's responsible and works hard."

"I hate it that Levi's mom isn't around," Laney said.

"Yeah, she wasn't cut out for ranch life."

Laney crumbled up the paper from the pastry. "I can't imagine why. I love it here."

Micah gave her that heart-stopping grin, and she wanted to melt into a puddle on the floor.

"You're special, and I'm glad you came here. I don't know what I thought about all day before you showed up."

He was thinking about her! She wanted to leap out of her seat and do a happy dance. He couldn't just leave her hanging. She had to know more. "You've been thinking about me?"

Micah reached over and brushed a hand down her bruised cheek. "I haven't stopped."

A loud alarm startled her, and she jumped.

They'd been so close and so quiet before the jarring noise.

Micah reached into his pocket. "Sorry. That's my phone." He looked at the screen and said, "It's Jameson. I'll call him back."

"No, no. It's okay. You can take it," Laney said.

"I guess I need to get going. If he's calling to give me something else to do, I might be up half the night in the office." He stood and shoved the phone back into his pocket.

"Okay. Thanks for keeping me company. I think Dixie fell asleep." Sure enough, the border collie was curled up on the floor beside the recliner.

"She makes curling up by the fire look comfortable."

Laney felt a rush of heat fill her face at the thought of curling up in front of the fireplace with Micah. "Yeah. She does."

"I'll see you in the morning," he said as he opened the door.

"See you. Good night," she called out after him.

"Good night, Laney." His words were as sweet as honey and left her feeling light as air.

When she closed the door behind him, Dixie woke and whined.

"You need to go out, girl?" Laney opened the door, and Dixie bounded off the porch.

Laney left the door cracked, and Dixie returned a few minutes later.

"What do you think about sleeping over?" Laney asked.

When Dixie didn't protest, Laney made sure the fire was built up enough to last at least part of the night and got ready for bed. With nothing else to do, she could call it an early night.

When she slid beneath the covers half an hour later, Dixie followed her to the bed.

"Nope. You're dirty. Not on the bed. At least not until we can figure out how to keep you clean for more than an hour."

Laney opened a closet and found a blanket folded on the top shelf. She left it folded a few times and made a bed for Dixie beside hers.

Once she was tucked in again, Laney picked up her phone to set the alarm. A barrage of notifications from Devin greeted her, and her heart sank. Her phone plan was linked to Devin's, and she wondered if he hadn't turned her coverage off just so he could harass her every day.

She quickly set the alarm and locked the phone. She could go into town on Sunday and get a prepaid phone.

Laney lay in the dark room with only the moon shining dimly through the window. She'd had a wonderful evening with Micah, and her happiness had been stripped from her at the sight of the messages from Devin. She hated that he was affecting her from so far away. She could be happy here if only he would leave her alone.

Another worry latched on in her mind. It had been two weeks since she'd left him, and his efforts to get a response from her hadn't diminished. Would he ever let her go?

She had to believe he would give up eventually. She had no intention of going back to him. Before, his threats that he would find her hadn't mattered because she didn't have anything to lose.

Only now she did have something to lose—her job, the cozy cabin, the Hardings.

Micah. The mere thought of losing him constricted her throat until she couldn't breathe.

Dixie whined and rested her chin on the bed beside Laney.

"It's okay, girl. I'm okay." She *wasn't* okay, but maybe if she said the words enough, someday they would become true.

CHAPTER 12
MICAH

Micah parked behind the main house just before suppertime. His nose crinkled at the smell of wet cattle. He really needed a shower. The bottle calf had fought him this morning during its feeding, and he'd slipped in a mud puddle. At least he hoped it was mud.

In a quick decision, he jumped out of the truck and headed inside to wash up as best he could in the bathroom in the back of the house. If he was lucky, he could find Laney in the kitchen and sneak her away for a few minutes alone. He'd been seeking her out more and more over the last week, and if her bright smiles were any indication, she was just as excited to see him.

After scrubbing all the way up his forearms, Micah found Laney in the kitchen running back and forth from one counter to the other. His mother darted out of the pantry with a handful of crackers and rushed into the meeting room.

Laney wore a light-colored apron over a thick sweater with the sleeves pushed up to her elbows. Her hair was bunched into a ball on top of her head, leaving the smooth skin of her neck exposed. He had the undeniable urge to brush his lips over the pale skin.

He cleared his throat and forced his thoughts to stay off Laney's tempting skin. "Something smells good."

Laney looked up as if she hadn't noticed he'd come in. "Hey. It's soup night."

"My favorite." At least the smell of the food over-powered the stench of animals.

"Which one?" Laney asked as she shoved a ladle into the chili.

"Chicken noodle."

Laney turned to him with a grin as if his answer was surprising.

"It was always my favorite," he added. "Mom made it for me almost every day when I was young."

"That's sweet," Laney said as she turned to grab another ladle.

"What can I help with?" It wasn't the quality time he'd had in mind, but Laney wasn't one to slack on the job. The least he could do was help.

"Grab that slow cooker." She pointed to a black one on the edge of the counter.

"You got it, boss." Micah grabbed the slow cooker that was filled to the rim with what looked like beef stew.

"We have a full house tonight, and the Erwins have been out riding all day. They're starving." She grabbed a handful of dish towels and a large bowl of shredded cheese and led the way.

As soon as she opened the door leading to the meeting room, he understood what all the fuss was about. Almost everyone at the ranch was already lined up. So much for being early.

He accepted instructions from Laney and his mother until supper was ready to be served. Laney hung back in the corner, waiting for the guests to get their fill first. After a few minutes, Micah took her by the hand and led her to stand with him at the back of the line.

Laney told him about her day as they made their way through the line, filling their bowls with soup and toppings. She gestured with her hands as she told him about helping his mother make the soups. She spoke quickly in her excitement, and he found himself distracted by the soft curve of her lips as she spoke.

At the table, the Erwins talked about their horse riding adventure with Maddie, and Levi entertained everyone with a story about finding a rattlesnake in the hay barn.

As soon as she'd finished her soup, Laney stood

and grabbed the empty bowls in front of Levi, Haley, and Mama Harding before disappearing into the kitchen. The Erwins and the Jacksons hung around for a few minutes, planning the next day's activities.

Micah pulled his compact notebook and pencil from his pocket and flipped it open to the latest page of ranch duties. "Okay, what's the status on the baler disks?"

"Gonna be in on Tuesday," Asher said.

"What about the fences?" Micah asked without looking up from his list.

"Checked the south pasture just before supper," Hunter said.

Micah made notes and crossed off completed tasks. "The new horse?"

"It'll be here tomorrow morning. They stopped for an extra day in Omaha," Lucas said.

Micah cleared his throat. "Tomorrow, we need to check the irrigation to the south pasture."

"Got it," Aaron said.

Making his way down the list, Micah noted who was responsible for each task. "That's everything."

"Wait a minute. What are you doing?" Lucas asked.

Micah frowned at his youngest brother. He never shared his own duties with everyone. He just reserved the tasks he didn't want to delegate for himself. Did they think he was slacking?

"Why do you care?" Micah asked.

"Just read the list," Lucas groaned.

Micah started at the top and spat out his list of chores. When he was finished, Asher held up a finger. "I'll fill up the fuel truck and order the new feed while I'm in town."

"I'll check the cattle," Noah said.

Hunter chimed in. "I'll mix the feed."

Micah's irritation grew. "What is this about?"

"Maddie told me you need the day off, so we're clearing your calendar," Lucas explained.

"I don't think so. I don't take days off."

Lucas groaned. "Come on. Just this once."

"Camille agreed," Noah added. "She said you've been making heart eyes at Laney for weeks, and you need to pick up the pace." Noah held up his hands. "Her words, not mine."

"I—" Micah started to protest.

"She said it would do both of you some good," Noah added.

"I agree," his mother chimed in as she swept past Micah to grab his empty bowl. "Laney is working hard and so are you. We don't want her to get burnt out before the busy summer season. Show her around. She hasn't even been out on the ranch yet. She's been working since she got here."

Micah rubbed his chin as he mulled over the idea. He didn't like the idea of taking the day off when he wasn't sick or injured, but spending the day with Laney was too tempting to pass up.

"When was the last time you took a day off?" Lucas asked. "I'll let you know when the new horse gets here, and you can bring her by the stables to see him."

"Now isn't the time to slack off. The wedding is next weekend, and you know we won't be fit for anything," Micah said.

"What does it matter? Everything will still get done tomorrow," Aaron added.

Micah huffed. His responsibilities warred with his desire to spend a whole, uninterrupted day with Laney. "Fine." He pushed off the table and shoved the list back into his pocket. "Just this once. I'm not making a habit of taking days off."

"We know, boss," Lucas said. "No one ever accused you of slacking."

Everyone disbanded, and Micah was left chewing over the change of plans. He liked having his hands in every piece of the ranch business. It was his responsibility, and he took it seriously.

But he was quickly warming up to the idea of a day alone with Laney. Hadn't he been wishing for more time with her? His excitement grew as he thought about telling her they both had the day off.

What if she didn't want to spend the day with him? Was it a date if you hung out together all day? Would she think it was a date? He mulled over ways to broach the subject with her and make his intentions known while making it clear that she could flat-out turn him down if she wanted. He wasn't prepared for a rejection from Laney, but he'd man up and take it like a kick to the gut if it came down to it.

He stepped into the kitchen looking for Laney and found his mother washing dishes in the deep sink.

"Where's Laney?" he asked.

"Camille gave her a ride home."

"Oh, okay. Are you sure you're okay with her taking the day off tomorrow?"

His mother rinsed the suds from her hands and wiped them on the dish towel. "I'm sure. We don't have anyone checking out or in tomorrow, and the menus are easy."

He leaned against the counter beside her. "I don't know about this. What if something goes wrong tomorrow?"

"Well, they'll know how to get in touch with you. You need to loosen your grip on some things around here. Your dad will be around, and he hasn't forgotten how to keep this place running."

"You're right. I know that."

His mother leaned her hip against the counter beside him and propped her hand on the other. "You do a fine job of running this place, son. But sometimes, people need to come first."

Micah hung his head. "I don't want to let anyone down. A lot of people are depending on me."

"We all know that, but we all have the same

strong responsibility to this place. It's our home. Don't you think we care too?"

"I know you do. You and Dad taught me how important it is to be dependable."

His mother patted his cheek like she'd done when he was a kid. "And we did a great job. You turned out just fine."

"Thanks."

"But you need to learn how to put as much effort into your relationship as you do your job. They both need to be cared for if you're going to be happy."

Micah chuckled. "Don't let me get away with anything."

"I don't intend to. You're my boy, and I love you, but I love Laney too. She needs all of us in different ways, and by the way she looks at you, I think she needs you the most."

Micah lowered his head and stuck his hands into his pockets. "I'm not sure I know how to make a relationship work."

"That's because you've always put the ranch at the top of the list. If you put God first and your relationship behind it, the rest will fall into place." She gave him a look full of pity and love. "What are you working for if it isn't to be happy with the ones you love?"

Micah shook his head. "I don't know."

"Figure it out, son. Laney needs more than a half-hearted try."

"No argument there," Micah said as he pushed off the counter. "I need to go see if she is even interested in spending the day with me first."

Mama Harding swatted at him with the dish towel. "Oh, I don't think you have to worry about that."

"Her last boyfriend hit her. I doubt it'll be easy to follow that."

His mother pursed her lips. "She knows you're a good man. She needs someone that she doesn't have to be afraid of, and I think that's you."

Micah sighed. He had a long row to hoe with Laney, and he didn't want to mess things up before they even got started. "Thanks, Mama. Let me know if you need help."

"I'll do no such thing. I've got it covered here. Go have your fun."

"Good night," Micah said as he crossed the kitchen.

"Night, son. I love you."

"Love you too." He tried to slow his steps as he made his way to the back door. Hope and fear fought within him, and he wouldn't know which would win the battle until he talked to Laney.

CHAPTER 13
LANEY

Laney was getting spoiled. She was used to twelve-hour workdays, but relaxing on the couch with a book in front of a cozy fire hadn't been a part of her after-work routine before. Some days she read a book, some days she talked to Dixie and moved things around until they were exactly where she wanted them to be, and some days she fell asleep on the couch with Dixie beside her. Blackwater Ranch felt like an extended vacation with all of the best accommodations and services.

Her eyelids were getting heavy as she scanned the words in the latest book she'd borrowed from the main house library. The smart thing to do would be to stick Micah's business card between the pages before she fell asleep.

A knock at the door jolted her out of the half-sleep state. Dixie was on her feet beside Laney in an instant.

"Easy, girl. You're as jumpy as me." She was finally getting used to the tight-knit security here. No stranger would be showing up at her door with Micah's cabin beside hers. His brothers, as well as Hunter and Maddie, were within throwing distance too.

Laney rubbed her drowsy eyes and said, "Coming." She didn't bother to hide Dixie anymore. Micah had approved of her nightly visitor.

Laney pressed her ear against the door and said, "Who is it?"

"Just me." Micah didn't bother to clarify who "me" was anymore.

She'd hoped he would stop by once he finished up his work for the evening. She'd asked Camille for a ride home earlier, not wanting to bother Micah while their evening meeting ran a little late.

Laney opened the door wide and gestured for him to enter. "Hey."

"Hey." Micah stuck his hands in his pockets. "Um, I didn't get to say good night."

Her mouth fell open at the sweetness of his words. "Did you come to tell me good night?" Laney whispered.

Micah scratched the back of his head. "Yes. I mean, no."

His fidgeting was making her nervous. What had him so wound up?

"Is everything all right?" she asked.

"Yes. I actually wanted to tell you that you have the day off tomorrow."

Her blood turned cold. "Why? Did I do something wrong?" She'd been working for almost a month now. Had they decided to let her go?

"No, nothing is wrong. You just have the day off." Micah's gaze fell to her feet. "I do too."

"Really? Why?" she asked, still unsure why she was being given time off so soon after starting a new job.

"I haven't taken time off in a while, and Mom said she and Haley have everything covered at the main house. No check-outs or check-ins. They just thought we could use some time—"

"*They,* as in?" Laney asked.

"Everyone." Micah shrugged.

She squinted at him. "I don't follow."

He held out a hand, palm up, and quickly asked, "Would you like to spend the day with me tomorrow? Like, a day date. I mean, a date that lasts... all day." He scratched the back of his head. "You know what I'm saying, right? I know this sounds forward, and I don't want you to think you're obligated to say yes at all. I just would like to get to know you better."

Laney bit her lips between her teeth. Micah was asking her on a date! Her heartbeat raced, and her face felt hot.

"There isn't some kind of rule about dating the boss?" She'd wondered if that was the reason he hadn't pressed for anything more with her. He seemed interested in her, but nothing had come of it until now.

Micah bounced the heel of his boot against the toe of the other. "We don't have any official rules about that here. We just have to keep working together if you get tired of me."

"Why would I get tired of you?" Laney asked.

"You know what I mean. You won't lose your job if you tell me to hit the road, and I won't give you a raise because you're gorgeous and I want to kiss you."

Laney's eyes widened. He wanted to kiss her!

"Yes. I definitely want to spend the day with you tomorrow." Any sleepiness she'd been fighting moments ago was long gone. She might not sleep a wink tonight if her heart kept racing.

Dixie barked behind Laney, and she laughed. "Dixie accepts your invitation as well."

Micah's expression relaxed into an easy smile. "Good. What time should I pick you up in the morning?"

"Usual time?" Laney offered.

"I'll be here. Good night." He tipped his imaginary hat to her and stepped off the porch into the dark Wyoming night.

"Good night."

She closed the door and pressed her open palms against it. Dixie danced in a circle just behind her, and Laney couldn't decide what to feel.

She turned around and asked, "You know anything about getting ready for a date?"

Dixie turned and trotted back to her cozy place by the fire.

Laney sighed. "That's what I was afraid of."

"What is that?" Laney asked when Haley pulled another compact from the bottomless makeup bag.

"Just some bronzer. Trust me, I won't make you look like a clown," Haley said.

"Oh, I know. I just won't be able to replicate this look." Laney's eyes were expertly lined, and her cheeks were contoured—something she'd only heard of in passing until today.

"Micah is going to lose his mind. I know Micah likes you even without makeup, so I kept it subtle. Now that the bruise is gone, you really don't need anything."

"Thanks. I'm so nervous." Laney shook her sweaty palms.

"Don't be!" Haley moved to stand behind Laney and lifted her hair. "How do you want your hair? I think it looks great like it is."

Laney studied her reflection in the old mirror. "Let's just leave it. No use setting him up for an expectation I can't maintain."

"Yes! Be yourself," Haley agreed.

There was a knock at the door, and Laney moved to answer it.

"Hold up, speedy. Let me find the lipstick." Haley rummaged through her Mary Poppins bag and mumbled to herself.

"He's at the door."

Haley lifted her attention to Laney. "I know, but if he can sit in the woods for hours at dawn hunting, he can wait two minutes for his date to finish getting ready." She held up a tube of neutral-colored lipstick. "Found it!"

"I really don't need that," Laney said.

"Oh, yes you do. You're getting smooched today. I can feel it."

"You can feel my smooches? That's weird."

Haley handed her the tube. "Put it on."

Laney begrudgingly accepted the tube and slid it over her lips. "There. All done?"

"Yes. You're dismissed."

She handed the lipstick back to Haley. "Thanks for this."

"Don't mention it." Haley wrapped Laney in a

quick hug before shoving her out of the tiny bathroom.

Laney hustled to the door and fought the urge to fling it open and seem too eager. Taking a deep breath, she opened it slowly.

She'd known it would be Micah, but she hadn't expected her date to steal her breath. He wore a dark-gray thermal shirt that stretched tight over his muscular arms, camo pants, and a clean pair of work boots. His mouth tugged to one side in a playful grin that had butterflies dancing in her stomach.

He pulled a hand from behind his back and offered her a small bouquet of yellow flowers. "Good morning."

Shock kept her from responding immediately, but she was able to offer a garbled "Good morning," as she accepted the flowers. She had no idea what they were called and didn't care. She would be naming each one of them after their date. Tears welled in her eyes, begging to release the emotions swirling within her, and she blinked rapidly.

"Thank you. I'll put these in a glass." She quickly turned away from him and strode into the kitchen to hide. The little that she'd worked herself ragged for or that others had given her was the most she'd ever had. Pretty things like flowers had always been out of her reach.

Haley marched through the cabin and out the door with a wave. "See you later, kids. Have fun!"

Laney yelled toward the door, "Call Micah if you need me. I'm leaving my phone here."

"We're not calling you!" Haley yelled back.

Micah stepped inside and closed the door. He slowly made his way into the kitchen where Laney arranged the flowers in a mason jar. "I didn't realize spending time with you would cause such a stir around here."

The fresh smell of pine tingled her nose as he came to stand beside her. She was going to have a hard time keeping her head clear today with him so close.

"Haley called me five minutes after you left last night."

"She's a busybody," Micah said, but his accusation lacked the sting of malice.

Laney chuckled. "That she is. She'll be sure to let everyone know you were a gentleman and brought me flowers."

He inched closer, and she leaned toward him instinctually. Were they going to get to the smooching Haley had foretold already? Laney couldn't find the will to resist.

"You look beautiful," he whispered, as if the words were meant for her ears alone. A secret only they shared.

"Thank you," she whispered back. "You look handsome too."

"I don't think I have ever stayed completely

clean for a full day. We'll see how long this lasts."

A pang of guilt pinched her heart. If it weren't for her, he would be out working now. And if she were honest, she loved his dedication to the ranch and his family. Few people were as dependable as Micah Harding. The gravity of what he was giving her today wasn't lost on her. It was a valuable gift when a responsible man like Micah put everything aside to spend time with her.

"What are we doing first?" she asked.

"I was thinking we could get breakfast at Sticky Sweets. You could get a fancy coffee drink and one of those desserts you like."

Laney couldn't contain the grin that spread across her face. "That sounds perfect."

"Then I can show you around town while we wait for the surprise."

"A surprise!" She almost squealed. "I love surprises."

Micah chuckled. "You can have them all. I'm not much for surprises myself."

"Oh, Haley warned me you didn't like surprises," Laney said.

Micah shook his head. "I'm never going to live that one down, am I?"

"Probably not."

Micah offered her his arm. "I'll just have to make sure you get all the surprises then."

Laney looped her arm around his and nestled herself at his side. "I won't argue with that."

CHAPTER 14
MICAH

Micah opened the door of Sticky Sweets Bakery for Laney to enter first. The aroma of sugar and freshly baked bread hit him in the face, and his stomach began to cry for sustenance. He rarely had the chance to stop by the bakery. If work brought him into town for an extended amount of time, he usually skipped a meal.

Laney closed her eyes as she inhaled the sweet smell. "I could eat my weight in pastries right now."

Micah pointed at the menu on the wall behind the counter. "Have at it. I've got my eye on a breakfast sandwich."

When they reached the counter, Laney ordered a sausage, egg, and cheese croissant, a puff pastry, and a caramel latte. Micah got the breakfast sandwich and black coffee before adding a few extra sandwiches to go for their lunch.

After Micah paid and they both stepped out of the line, he motioned toward the cafe seating area. "You want to get us a table? I'll wait for our order."

Laney grabbed a handful of napkins, two forks, and two packets of jelly before choosing a two-seater table in the corner of the room.

Micah was busy watching Laney when someone grabbed his arm.

"Hey, you. I haven't seen you in a few weeks," Olivia said as she wrapped her arms around his neck.

Micah leaned forward, hunched down to her shorter height and careful not to allow her to plaster herself against him from chest to thigh. He tried to remind himself that Olivia was overly friendly with everyone, and she didn't realize how uncomfortable she made him when she full-on hugged him.

When she released him, she brushed her short, black hair behind her ear.

"Olivia. How are you?" Micah asked, a little stunned by her assault. He hoped this conversation didn't go the way of all the others.

"I'm great. I haven't seen you since Asher's wedding. Speaking of weddings, Noah and Camille's wedding is next week. Do you have a date?"

Yep. Just like every other time he ran into Olivia Lawrence. "I do." He didn't actually have a date yet, but he had intended to ask Laney. He just kept forgetting to do the asking.

Olivia's shoulders sank. "Oh. Well, I was hoping to catch you before someone else snagged you."

"Sorry. I intend to go with Laney. She's helping out at the ranch." Micah pointed out Laney who watched him and Olivia from the table.

Laney's expression told him she was uncomfortable, and he could probably guess why. Olivia was a cross between a flirt and a happy little pixie with her friendly personality. He could only guess what her greeting had looked like to Laney.

"Oh. Mama mentioned you hired a new housekeeper," Olivia said.

He really hoped the demeaning undertone in Olivia's words was unintentional. "She's been a lifesaver lately."

Olivia raised a timid hand to wave at Laney. "Good to hear."

The barista shouted a coffee order, and Olivia reached for her drink. "I'll see you soon." She turned and left the bakery without looking his way again.

His and Laney's order was up next, and he balanced the tray of food and drinks as he joined Laney at their table.

"Who was that?" Laney asked. "I mean, I haven't met her."

Micah dealt out their orders and placed the tray on the empty table beside theirs. "That was Olivia Lawrence. Her family runs the Lawrence farm next door."

"Right. Mama Harding told me about them. She said you trade with them sometimes."

"We do." Micah sat and said, "I'd like to return thanks."

"Oh, yes. Go ahead," Laney said, bowing her head and closing her eyes.

"Father, thank You for providing another meal for us. We pray that You would go with us through this day and help us to get to know one another. Amen."

Micah lifted his head and squirmed in his seat. "Um, Olivia asked me if I had a date to Noah and Camille's wedding."

Laney's eyes widened, and a splotchy redness crept up her neck. "Okay. Are you going to go with her?"

He rubbed the palms of his hands on his pants. "Actually, I told her I wanted to go with you. I know I haven't asked you yet, and I should have thought of this before now, but things like wedding dates slip my mind."

Laney slowly relaxed. It was as if he could see the tension leaving her body with her long exhale.

Micah continued, "So, would you like to go with me? I mean, I know you're already planning to go, but would you be my date? I'm not really sure what having a date to a wedding is like, so you might need to let me know if there is some etiquette protocol that I need to know about."

Laney laughed as he nervously spilled his guts. "I'd love to go with you as your date."

"Perfect." He'd have to ask Haley later if something like a corsage was necessary. He'd done an excellent job of ignoring formalities up until now, and he might need some tips.

By the time Laney picked up her puff pastry, they had both gotten over the awkwardness and tension of running into Olivia.

Laney bit into her dessert and moaned. "Oh wow. This is even better than before."

Micah added a new task at the top of his to-do list: Make sure Laney had all the puff pastries she could ever want. If dessert could make her this happy, he'd buy stock in Sticky Sweets. "I added a few sandwiches we can eat for lunch. I have another surprise."

She leaned over the table, eager for more hints. "What is it?"

Micah gathered their trash and piled it on the empty tray. "What fun would the surprise be if I told you? That's not how it works."

She bounced in her seat like a kid. "Oh, I can't wait. I'm too excited."

He tried to hide his knowing grin as he stood to take their tray to the trash. "I haven't gotten the call that it's ready yet, so I thought I could show you around town while we wait."

"Sure! Camille pointed out a few things when I

first came here, but the only other place I know about is the grocery store. Your mom sent me to pick up a few things once."

He reached for her hand as they exited the bakery, and she accepted it without hesitation. They had fallen into a comfortable companionship already. He hoped this was an indication of how the rest of the day would go.

The mid-April sky was clear and blue over Blackwater with only a moderate chill. Once they were settled in the truck, Laney rolled the passenger window down and leaned on the door as he pointed out shops and landmarks around the small town. He showed her the post office and the hardware store on the far side of town before making their way back through the courthouse square and stopping at Grady's Feed and Seed.

He parked in the lot to the side of the warehouse. "We do a lot of business with Grady, so I think this is a good time to introduce you in case you need to pick up anything for the ranch."

"I've heard you talk about Grady's in the meetings before."

Micah rounded the truck and offered a hand to Laney as she stepped out. "He's been a family friend my whole life. He pretty much knows what we're looking for by now."

She didn't release his hand, and he felt a swelling in his chest as they entered the store together. Holding hands with a woman was an elementary step, but it held a deep significance with Laney. Micah had never been one to publicly display affection, but he felt pride lifting his shoulders with her beside him.

They found Grady in the boot section wrapping up a conversation with another older man. When he spotted Micah holding hands with Laney, the white-haired man grinned beneath his beard.

"Look what the cat dragged in." Grady gave Micah's hand a firm shake.

"How you doin', old timer?" Micah asked.

"Oh, I think I'll make it another day." Grady turned his attention to Laney. "Who is this? I don't think we've met."

Micah scooted closer to Laney. "This is Laney Parker. She's working at the ranch."

"Well, it's good to meet you. Looks like you've done a number on this old grouch," Grady said, pointing to Micah.

"I'm not a grouch," he said, praying he was telling the truth. Grady's jokes were all in good fun, but did everyone see him as a grump?

Grady looked to Laney for backup. "His bark is worse than his bite."

Laney turned to Micah with a smile that let him know she wasn't reading too much into Grady's taunts. "He hasn't tried to bite me yet."

And he wouldn't. He hoped Laney wasn't

thinking about the man who *had* done more than bite her. If he thought about her piece of trash ex, he'd ruin his mood for the rest of the day.

"He better not," Grady said. "I'll give him a run for his money."

Micah lifted a brow and gave Grady a half-hearted glare. "Anyone who comes at Laney has to go through me first."

Grady slapped a heavy hand on Micah's shoulder. "That's my boy. What can I do for you today?"

"I just wanted to introduce you to Laney. She'll be around a lot, and she might be stopping by."

Grady stuck his hands into the pockets of his overalls. "Well, you two sure brightened up my day. Come back and see me whenever you're in town."

"I will," Laney said. "It was nice to meet you."

Grady waved his good-byes as another customer led him to a different part of the store.

"He was nice," she said as they turned to walk back the way they came.

"Oh, yeah. Grady is one who would give you the shirt off his back. He's good to do business with too."

They walked around the rest of the store, and Micah told her about the things the ranch needed. When they came to the clothing section, he helped her pick out some of the better brands of workwear. When she'd picked out and tried on a coat and a pair of boots, he tucked them under his arm, and reached for her hand with the other.

"What are you doing?" she asked.

"I'm buying these for you. We might be outside a lot today, and you'll need these."

Laney tugged on his arm. "You don't have to do that. I can just stop by the cabin and grab a few more layers."

Micah shook his head. "It's a done deal. You'll get some good use out of these."

They walked in silence for a few moments before she moved in closer to his side. "Thank you. I really appreciate it."

He knew she did, and he wasn't worried about buying anything for her. She'd get a lot of use out of it, and he would feel much better knowing she was staying warm.

Micah paid for the coat and boots, and Laney slid her hand back into his. After spending the morning with her like this, his brothers were going to have to pry him away from her to make him work tomorrow. Nothing had ever diverted his attention from the ranch before, but he wanted this with Laney. Maybe this is what his mother had been trying to tell him when she said he needed to put as much effort into his relationship with Laney as he did his job. If this was what she'd meant, he could get behind the idea one hundred percent.

He opened the truck door for Laney, and a text

pinged on his phone. He quickly read the message from Lucas. "Looks like your surprise is ready."

"Really? Let's go!" Laney jumped into the truck and settled in her seat, ready to speed back to the ranch.

Micah chuckled at her eagerness. "Hold your horses. I'll get you there as quick as I can." Speaking of horses, what was she going to think about her surprise? He hoped she wasn't afraid of them. That might blow the plan up in his face.

Laney sat on the edge of her seat during the ride back to the ranch. He loved the childlike excitement that radiated from her. She watched as he drove past the main house.

"Where are we going?"

"I thought we could explore the ranch."

She tucked her hands under her thighs and raised her shoulders. "That sounds like fun."

"We have to make a stop at the stables first. Lucas and Maddie are keeping your surprise entertained."

"What is it?"

He parked in front of the stables and jumped out of the truck to meet her at the front. "You'll see." He instinctively reached for her hand, and she caught it as she picked up the pace to keep up with his long stride.

Micah pushed open the door to the stables and gestured for Laney to enter first. She slowed to take in the high ceilings and stalls. The other end of the building had a wide opening, and the morning sun cast its beams inside.

"I haven't been in here yet. This place is huge."

"Maddie can tell you all about it. What do you know about horses?"

"Um, I've seen them in some old westerns. It was all my dad ever watched on TV."

He picked up a hint of hesitation in her voice. She hadn't said much about her parents. And as much as he wanted to know the story behind their neglect, he forced the hand she was holding to relax. Her excitement was contagious.

Maddie stuck her head out of a stall halfway down the right side of the building. "I'm in here."

Micah picked up his pace to keep up with Laney who was now leading the way. "I know you haven't met any of the horses yet, but this one just arrived this morning. She's new, and I thought you'd like to meet her first."

"This is so fun!"

They reached the stall Maddie had yelled from, and Micah tugged on Laney's hand, urging her to stay back. "She's mucking right now, so you might not want to get too close."

Laney covered her nose. "Got it."

"I'm almost finished in here. Are you ready to meet Goldie?" Maddie asked.

"Goldie! That's such a cute name," Laney said.

"She's about six years old, so her previous owners gave her the name, but I'm with you. It's cute, and it suits her. Just wait till you see her." Maddie rested the shovel next to the wheelbarrow and pulled off her gloves. "She's right over here."

Micah and Laney followed Maddie to a stall near the back of the stables. When Laney saw Goldie through the bars of the stall, her hands jerked to her face. "She's gorgeous!"

Maddie leaned against the bars. "She's a Palomino. That's what we call the yellowish coat with a white tail and mane. I think she'll fit in here just fine."

"Wow." Laney's head tilted to the side as she gazed at the horse. "She's so big and pretty."

Micah leaned closer to Laney, unwilling to disturb her fascination with Goldie. "The ranch needed a new cutting horse. Those are the ones we use for herding, and Goldie has some training already. Lucas and Maddie are going to train her to know exactly what we do around here."

"Yep. She's our newest ranch hand," Maddie said.

"So I'm not the newest ranch hire anymore," Laney pointed out.

Micah nodded. "Looks like Goldie has you beat. I was thinking you might want to take a ride around the ranch today. It's okay if you'd rather take my truck."

"Yes! I mean, no. I don't want to take the truck. I want to ride" –she waved her hand toward Goldie— "the horses."

"Perfect." Micah grinned at Laney's agreement. "Goldie hasn't had enough time to get settled in yet, so I was thinking you could ride Skittle, and I'll be on Weston."

Laney gaped for a moment before asking, "Skittle and Weston? Those are their names?"

"Yep. Levi got to name Skittle. Guess his favorite candy."

Laney twisted her finger. "I have no idea how to ride a horse."

Maddie piped up. "Don't worry! We'll get you all set. Micah knows what to do, so you're in good hands."

Micah shrugged. "You trust me?"

Laney's gaze held his, unwavering and true. "I do."

And Micah knew something had shifted between them. Trust wasn't something he took lightly, and it had a deeper weight for Laney too. His new mission was to continue to prove to Laney that he would be by her side through anything.

For once, she wouldn't have to fight anything alone.

CHAPTER 15
LANEY

Laney sat atop the horse and forced her eyes to stay open. Before today, she wouldn't have admitted to a fear of heights, but she didn't realize how tall horses were until she was sitting atop Skittle.

"You comfortable?" Micah asked from a few feet below.

"As comfortable as I can be this far from the ground."

Micah rested a hand on her thigh, and she braved a look down at him.

"You're safe on Skittle. I'm right here with you. If you don't want to do this, we can still take the truck."

"No. I really want to ride. I'll be fine. I just need to get used to it."

"Remember everything I told you?" he asked.

"That's a tall order, cowboy. I'm having trouble focusing on more than staying on at this point."

He chuckled, and the deep sound settled the churning inside her. The blue sky was streaked with white clouds, and the air was warmer, signaling the changing of the season. It was a beautiful day to be outside, and the unknown reaches of the ranch called to her.

"Let me grab our lunch from the truck. I'll be right back." Micah strode off toward the other side of the stables.

"I can do this," Laney said to Skittle. "You won't throw me off or anything, right?"

Skittle stayed obediently still, waiting for a command to move.

"I'm new at this. Think you could go easy on me?" she asked.

Skittle didn't move. Not so much as a twitch.

"You don't talk as much as Dixie."

As if summoned, Dixie ran around the side of the stables, followed by Micah carrying the bag of sandwiches. Skittle began to turn away from Dixie, and Laney gripped the reins.

"Wait. Where are we going?" Laney asked. Once again, Skittle didn't respond.

"She's familiar with Dixie, but it might take her a minute to get used to her being around." Micah lifted himself onto Weston who stood calmly beside Skittle.

"Okay. Click your tongue and tell her to go," Micah said.

Laney clicked and gave the command with more authority than she felt. Skittle was definitely in control here, and the knowledge wasn't lost on Laney.

Within seconds, Skittle had settled into a rhythmic walk, and Laney grew accustomed to the shakes and moves of the horse.

"You okay?" Micah asked.

"I think so. This isn't so bad."

"This is about as exciting as it gets."

Laney breathed a sigh of relief. "Good. I can handle this."

"I thought we could check out the south pasture first, so you can see the cows, then we can make our way back here along the perimeter. We might be able to make it to Bluestone Creek this afternoon."

"I'd love to see that. Everything is so beautiful out here."

About an hour later, they stopped to eat lunch at a creek that bordered the north side of the southern pasture. She'd seen the cattle, and they'd run into Aaron and Levi who were putting out the feed. Dixie hadn't strayed too far from them, though she ran ahead from time to time.

The open air and the quietness fascinated her. She was used to working in a loud and rowdy bar, and Micah worked here, in the wide-open spaces where her mind could wander and dream.

Micah helped her dismount from Skittle, and they tied the horses to a nearby tree.

"The sky is so blue today," Laney said as she accepted her sandwich from Micah.

Micah looked up and shrugged. "I can't ever tell. I'll have to trust you when you say it's blue."

"Oh, I forgot you're colorblind. Is it that bad?"

"It could be worse. The colors I see are so muted that they all look similar. I'm not fully blind to the variations, but they're sometimes hard to distinguish."

She unwrapped her sandwich and felt a pang of hurt that Micah couldn't enjoy the beautiful colors of nature. "That sounds awful. I guess I take colors for granted."

"It's not that bad. I have the most problem with red, and I can usually figure out the rest. I have an app on my phone that helps when I'm not sure."

Laney threw her head back in a loud and uninhibited laugh. "You're joking! There's an app for that."

"I'm very serious. It's humiliating when I have to use my smartphone to make sure I cut the right wire."

"I had no idea. I'm having trouble comprehending all of the limitations of being color blind."

"I'm used to it. My mom has some problems too, but mine is worse."

She looked around and thought about all that he was missing. "There's so much."

"Tell me about it," he said.

"Like, describe the colors?"

"Yeah. What do they look like to you?"

Laney looked around for anything that she could explain to him. "The sky is like water. Not just like the color that looks like water sometimes, but it's... cool and calm."

Micah watched her as she looked around. "Okay. What else?"

She touched the grass where they sat. It extended around them in every direction like an ocean. "Green is like... I don't know. Food? Lots of foods are green." She laughed and scratched her head.

"Most green foods are bold enough that I can tell," Micah said.

Laney looked at him, and a realization struck her in the heart. She didn't want him to miss something as beautiful as color, and as difficult as it was to describe the things he couldn't see, she knew she'd keep trying. She wanted to give him everything, and the enormity of that thought was frightening and freeing at the same time.

"Your eyes are green," Laney whispered. "Mine are too."

Micah stared into her eyes as if he could read the beatings of her heart without translation. She was falling for him, and it felt more like being knocked off her feet by a furious wind. Love had hit her square in the chest. It was new, it was big, and it was scary. But she knew that no one had ever accepted her—complete, flawed, and fragile—before now.

T heir ride after lunch was filled with Laney's questions and Micah's explanations. He told her about everything he did on the ranch and how they kept things running as smoothly as possible. It seemed as if "smooth" was a relative term because Micah made it sound like ranching was managing a series of unexpected setbacks.

They reached Bluestone Creek within a few hours, and they made it back to the stables just before sunset. Laney's behind was tired of being in the saddle, but seeing the ranch with Micah was something she wouldn't trade for anything. It had been a perfect day, and the best way to get to know each other.

"Camille is delivering our dinner to my cabin if you're not tired of me," Micah said as they handed their horses off to Lucas.

"That sounds perfect," Laney said as she wrinkled her nose. "Except I stink. Do I have time for a shower?"

"Sure. I'd like one too."

Back in his truck, Micah reached for her hand, and the contact felt like a level of safety she'd never known before. If he was beside her, she felt certain nothing could hurt her.

When they parked between their cabins, Dixie met Laney at her door.

"Sorry, girl. I have a date tonight."

Dixie whined as Laney slipped inside. She zipped through a quick shower and blew her hair dry. Going out in the cold with wet hair wasn't a good idea. She tidied up around the small cabin for five minutes before Micah knocked on her door.

She opened the door, and Dixie slipped in first. Laney huffed in shock.

Micah shrugged one shoulder. "She was here before me."

Laney stepped out of the doorway to let him in. "I thought it would be just the two of us."

"I can put her out if you want," he offered.

She waved a hand. "No, I don't have the heart to kick her out. I'll just build a fire, and she'll stay beside it."

Micah turned as headlights shone through the open door. "That's Camille. I'll grab our supper."

Laney bent to talk to Dixie. "Be good, okay. He's special. We don't want to run him off."

Dixie barked once.

"I knew you'd agree. Let's get your bed ready."

Laney had reserved a special blanket for her night-time friend, and she spread it in front of the fireplace.

Micah returned a minute later with arms filled with bags. "I think she sent enough to feed an army."

Laney reached for the bags. "Here. I'll get it ready."

Micah handed over the bags and rubbed his hands together. "I'll build a fire."

In the kitchen, Laney opened bowl after bowl of warm foods. They were having baked chicken, green beans, mashed potatoes, and corn on the cob. Camille even sent a slice of hot apple pie for dessert.

Micah stepped up beside Laney in the kitchen as she placed their drinks on the round, wooden table. "Something smells delicious."

"I know. Your mom sure knows how to cook."

When everything was ready, Micah blessed the food. They ate in silence for the next few minutes, and the ease of being with him warmed her from the cold day they'd spent on the ranch.

"It's so quiet. I'm not used to eating without everyone talking over each other," Micah said.

"I know. Especially Levi. He never stops talking," Laney recalled with a smile.

Micah pulled his phone from his pocket. "My phone hasn't rang once today. They were serious about giving us the day off."

"I've had a great day with you," Laney said.

Micah turned his attention to his food for a few seconds before looking back up at her. "I'm sorry about this morning with Olivia. I know it probably bothered you, but she's really just a family friend. We don't have a relationship history either, unless you count one date to prom."

The mention of Olivia made Laney uncomfortable, but the fact that he acknowledged her unease assured her. "I believe you. It bothered me a little bit at first because she was so friendly with you."

"That's just Olivia. We grew up living next door, so we've known each other all our lives. I didn't want you to think it was something more. I'm not seeing anyone else."

Laney sucked in a deep breath, determined not to get choked up over Micah's thoughtfulness. "Thank you. It means a lot that you're open and honest with me about things like that. I was with Devin for years, and I'm pretty sure he wasn't faithful. He would flirt with other women in front of me at the bar all the time. It was almost as if he wanted to show me he was desired by all the women fawning over him."

Micah put his fork down and scratched the back of his neck. "That's not right, Laney. You know that. You deserve better."

She swallowed hard and tried to continue. Micah was so easy to talk to, even when the subject was difficult to face. "I know. We had been together for so long that I didn't realize how bad things were until it was too late. It was almost like things happened so slowly that I didn't notice. Looking back now, I can't believe I was so blind."

"Why were you with him in the first place?" Micah asked.

Laney huffed. "Years ago, I was working at a sports bar, and Devin came in with a big group of men all wearing nice suits and ordering top-shelf drinks. They were seated in my section, and Devin kept pulling me to his side. He was forward and charming, and he asked for my number. He called me later, and we started seeing each other. Soon after, he convinced me to come work at the bar he owned. I liked my job, but he was adamant that I would like his bar better.

"I moved in with him soon after I changed jobs, and he would always praise my hard work. When I did better, he gave me more hours. The hours continued to creep up until I was working all the time. Our place was close to the bar, so I was there most hours of the day and night. Work was my life.

"When we lived and worked together, I felt as if I didn't have a way out. It was my life, and it wasn't like I had parents to go back to."

"What's the deal with your parents? Why aren't they around?" Micah asked.

Laney sat back in her chair, afraid to tell him

everything. If her parents hadn't cared about her, how could anyone else?

"Some people aren't cut out to be parents. They weren't abusive or anything, but I always felt like a burden. I moved out when I graduated from high school, and I could feel their relief."

Micah narrowed his eyes at her. "I don't understand."

"There isn't much to know. I don't think they ever wanted kids. I've been gone for eight years now, and I call them every so often when I think about them. Sometimes they answer, and sometimes they don't return my calls." Laney shook her head. "It isn't like I ever called to say anything important. I guess I feel like I should check on them every once in a while. Dad has some health problems, and I worry about him."

Micah reached over and laid a hand on her fidgeting fingers. "How they treated you isn't a reflection of your worth. I care about you. My family cares about you. And you'll always have a home here."

Laney stared at his hand covering hers. The comfort Micah offered felt foreign and scary, but she desperately wanted to rest her head on his chest and cry. She felt the tears welling in her eyes now.

As if the scared child she'd once been was allowed to speak for the first time, the words spilled from her mouth on jerky breaths. "It hurts when someone you love doesn't love you back."

Micah stood and pulled her up from where she sat. She fell into his arms and cried on his chest. She wanted to stop—begged the tears to leave. This day with Micah was supposed to be a new beginning, and she was scaring him off with her pity party.

"It's okay. Let it out. Get it all out of your system now because they don't deserve your tears. You have a family here if you want it."

Her sobs hit their second wind. She couldn't understand his acceptance, couldn't comprehend his kindness. She wanted to let the old hurt go more than anything, but she'd lived with it so long that it felt like a part of her heart—the heavy, black bottom.

When her well had run dry and she'd spent all of her tears, Micah brushed a hand over her hair, soothing her like a child. Funny, she couldn't remember her own parents comforting her.

"Your parents aren't here now. I am. And I'm not going anywhere."

She could hear his words beside her ear, but the deep timbre vibrated his chest that was flush with her body. She felt his promise in her bones and veins. His vow was strong and unwavering.

"And all that time he spent tearing you down, I was praying, begging God to send you to me. I needed you. I wanted you. I just didn't know your name yet."

She buried her face in his shirt and closed her eyes. She'd never been held like this by a man. It was a peace like she'd never known before. "I'm so glad I ended up here."

Micah squeezed her tighter. "Me too."

She breathed the most life-giving breath of her life and raised her head to him. She'd seen him lead the ranch with a gruffness that couldn't be denied. She'd seen him change gears and adapt to new circumstances in half a second. And now, she was seeing the soft, understanding side of the work-worn man. He saved this part of himself for her.

He brushed the calloused pads of his thumbs over her cheeks, wiping away tears of sorrow that now spilled in happiness. "The first time I saw you, I knew you were going to change my life. I don't mean love at first sight. I just knew you were important, and you are."

He thought she had changed his life? She was the one who had come to him broken and crawling on skinned knees. He lifted her up and gave her a reason to fight for the life she'd stumbled into here at Blackwater Ranch.

The look of adoration in his eyes turned to desire, and she felt the pull toward him. Every cell in her body was drawn to him like a magnet. Her skin hummed at his nearness, begging for the connection she craved.

His gaze fell to her mouth, and his jaw tightened. His hand slid around her waist as the other brushed against the side of her neck and up into her hair.

The strength in his hands was terrifying and exhilarating. He harnessed ten times her strength in those hands, and yet the pressure against her back and neck was used for good—to pull her closer to him.

A mere inch separated them, and the silence around them pulsed with the tension between them. Laney slid her hands up his arms, over his broad shoulders, and up his neck.

As if he'd been held back by a chain, his restraint broke and he claimed her mouth in a rush. He pulled her closer, and her body molded to his. All of the air in her lungs disappeared, and her ragged, nervous breaths were all that was left to sustain her as his lips moved against hers.

Micah broke the connection in a rush and took a step back. Gasping for air, he rubbed his hands over the back of his head. "Where's Dixie when I need a chaperone?"

Laney touched her tingling lips and fought to catch her breath. She didn't need a chaperone. She needed Micah.

She took a step toward him, but Micah held out a hand to keep the distance.

"No. I'm serious. I want to take things slow, so I need a few feet of space." He pushed the heels of his palms into his eyes. "Give me a minute to think about the national anthem or something."

A loud ringing came from another room, and Micah lifted his head. "Is that seriously the bedroom calling?"

Laney stifled a chuckle. She shouldn't find his restraint amusing. She was battling the same temptations. "It's my phone."

"Do you need to get that?" he asked.

"No. It's nothing." She would bet her paycheck it was Devin, and she definitely wasn't answering that call.

As soon as the ringing stopped, it began again.

"Are you sure you don't need to get that? It might be important."

"I'm sure." The ringing seemed to be getting louder, tightening all of the muscles in her body.

"You know who it is?" he asked.

Laney dropped her chin and nodded.

Micah kept his attention locked on her as the phone continued to ring. "Laney. What's going on?"

She fought against the fear that had been invading her dreams every night and said, "It's Devin."

"What are you talking about? I thought you said you left him."

"I did," she hurried to answer. "I'm not seeing him or anything, but he hasn't stopped calling since I left."

Micah turned toward the ringing in her bedroom. "You mean he calls you like this all the time? It's been over a month."

"I know. I just ignore the calls."

"What else has he been doing?" Fire burned in Micah's eyes as the realization sank in.

"Nothing. Just calling... and texting and leaving voicemails."

Micah strode for the bedroom, and Laney leapt to grab his arm. "What are you doing?"

"I'm putting a stop to it. He won't call you again after I set him straight."

"Please don't. You don't have to do that. I'll just ignore him." She spoke quickly as they neared the bedroom.

He turned around quickly, and she almost ran into him. "Laney, you don't have to put up with that. That's excessive. He's on his third call right now." He stood in the doorway and pointed toward the still-ringing phone.

"I'm just—" Laney began.

"Scared? Because I'm about to flip the roles here. He'll have a death wish before he dials your number again."

The phone silenced, and they both looked at it, waiting for it to begin its tune. When it didn't ring again, Micah sighed and turned to her.

"Listen, that's not going to fly around here. He can't harass you like that. I can either call him back right now and give him the new rules or we can go to the authorities and let them know about your history with this guy. Calling you multiple times a day for over a month is nuts."

"I don't want to go to the police," Laney said.

Micah rested his hands on her arms and rubbed gently. "I have a friend in the county police department. I'd feel much better if you let me tell him about this. Then there's some kind of record if he keeps it up. We're definitely figuring out how to block his calls."

"Okay. We can do all of that. I just don't want to let him know where I am."

He pulled her into his arms. "That makes two of us. Why didn't you tell me he was calling like this?"

"I didn't want to worry you. And I was afraid you'd kick me out."

Micah squeezed her tighter. Her lungs were begging for air. "I would never kick you out. I'll protect you from anything, even a crazy ex."

Laney chuckled. "That's good to know."

"We can talk to Haley about blocking him tomorrow. She'll know how to do that. And we'll get you a new phone number."

"Thank you." She'd been so afraid of his reaction, but now she felt relieved. She wasn't bearing the onslaught of Devin's attacks alone anymore.

He pulled back just enough to look down at her, and his kiss was softer and less urgent than the last time. This kiss was another vow—one that said he was willing to stand beside her through everything that came their way.

When they broke the kiss, she slid her hand to rest on his chest.

He laid his hand atop hers and slid a thumb along her jaw. "Do you feel what you do to me? You make my heart race, and I'm not sure it'll ever slow down now that you're here."

He was declaring himself to her with a commitment as strong and steady as a beating heart, and she knew she'd sleep soundly tonight knowing he was only steps away from her in the next cabin.

They cleaned up the rest of the dishes and said good night. Without a TV for entertainment, they both knew cuddling and kissing on the couch wasn't a good idea.

"We can talk to Camille and Haley tomorrow about this. They'll know what to do," Micah said.

Laney nodded. "I know. I should have gone to them sooner."

"I'll let you know when I get in touch with my friend at the police station. In the meantime, try to take someone with you if you have to go into town.

If I'm not around, Haley is usually at the main house."

"That's a good idea," Laney said.

"I know I'm being a little extreme, but we can't let him find you."

The memory of the hit she'd taken rushed into her mind. "I know."

He picked up her hand and squeezed it. "There's nothing to worry about. I'm right here, and I'll do anything to protect you."

Her shoulders relaxed, and she sighed. She had no doubt that Micah would keep her safe. If the phone calls were taken care of soon, she wouldn't have anything to worry about.

CHAPTER 16
MICAH

Micah barely slept after leaving Laney's cabin. Knowing her ex was relentless in his efforts to contact her rubbed him the wrong way. She'd been terrified when she'd arrived at the ranch, and that fear was valid. The thought of what Laney had endured never failed to boil his blood.

A deep chill permeated his cabin the next morning because he'd slept with his bedroom window open. He'd left Dixie at Laney's last night, but he wanted every advantage when it came to protecting Laney. He wouldn't be caught slacking.

The next morning came early and unwelcome after he'd spent the day before with Laney. He'd never been one to drag his feet in the morning, and today was no different. The sooner he got up and got to work, the sooner he could get back to Laney.

He had a newfound respect for her. She'd been

worse off than he'd realized when she showed up here, and he admired her strength. The way she kept going and refused to let her chin fall was admirable —amazing even. She carried a slew of heavy burdens from her parents' neglect to the string of mediocre jobs that had led her to a man who didn't have the decency to keep his hands off her.

She'd endured more than he could imagine. His own life had been a piece of cake. He appreciated his caring family more after learning that Laney hadn't known the same unwavering support from her own family. She'd come here ready to work, and her resolve hadn't faltered. He admired that kind of heart strength.

And after all she'd done to make the best of things, he refused to allow her ex to see her determination slip. Every time she thought about doubting herself or her worth, Micah would be there to remind her. He slipped on his boots and silently vowed to stand beside her and proudly raise her up for the rest of his days.

But first, he had work to do. The ranch didn't wait for daylight, and Micah didn't either.

He closed the door of his cabin in the quiet dark before dawn and hoped the roaring of his truck's diesel engine wouldn't wake Laney. He'd left Aaron in charge yesterday, and Micah studied the short list of morning duties. He could knock them out before breakfast.

An hour and a half later, he picked Laney up at her cabin. She greeted him with a quick kiss on the cheek.

"Good morning." She slipped her hand into his as she closed the door behind her.

"What a good morning it is. How did you sleep?"

Laney huffed a dramatic breath. "Like a log. I think that was the best sleep I've had in ages."

"That's what I like to hear." Micah opened the passenger door of his truck and waited for her to get settled before taking his place behind the wheel.

They burst into the main house hand-in-hand and sporting matching smiles. The day off had done wonders for them.

Laney chatted with a guest couple throughout breakfast, and Micah took the opportunity to catch up with his brothers, Hunter, Maddie, and Jameson. They all assured Micah that they'd handled everything without his micromanaging yesterday, and he wasn't sure whether he felt relieved or unneeded.

After breakfast, Laney caught his attention with a look, and she darted her questioning glance toward Camille and Haley. Laney hadn't mentioned talking to the other women about her problems with Devin this morning, and he'd been waiting for her to initiate the conversation.

At her signal, he followed Laney as she approached Camille and Haley. They all excused themselves to the living room where Laney told them about Devin's incessant calls.

Haley chimed in first with a look of disgust. "First of all, how rude. Second, we're definitely blocking him."

"Do you know how to do that?" Laney asked.

"For sure. And it's a good thing you don't have social media. One less thing to worry about."

Camille rested her chin on her fist in thought. "I have some ideas, but I'm not sure what the course of action should be, if any. Any court filings would alert him to your location."

"I definitely don't want to do that," Laney said.

"I think if you block the calls, he might give up. He doesn't have anything else to go on, right?" Camille asked.

"As far as I know. And I have to hope that he wouldn't leave the bar long enough to come after me. I'm not really sure why he's being so insistent. They had to have replaced me at the bar by now, and I know now that he never loved me."

Hearing Laney talking about love in context with another man did strange and awful things to Micah's insides. No way had that low-life loved her. Micah loved her, and that vow would never include hurting her.

He *did* love her. There wasn't a doubt in his mind that Laney was the woman for him, and with that commitment came his unwavering loyalty. His devotion to Laney was only surpassed by his commitment to the Lord.

"You don't need anything from town, do you?" Camille asked.

"Um, maybe an alarm clock," Laney said.

"I'll get it," Micah said. "I have to go into town today anyway."

Camille nodded. "Perfect. I think Laney should stick to the ranch for a bit. At least until we see if anything happens after we block Devin's calls."

Micah turned to Laney. "Is this okay with you?"

"Of course. I don't need anything in town that someone couldn't pick up for me," Laney said.

"In that case, I'm going to call my buddy, Asa, and fill him in," Micah said. "He's a police officer, and I'd feel better knowing he was in the loop at least."

Camille piped up. "Oh, yeah. I think that's a good idea." She turned to Laney. "We went to school with Asa. He's a good one to have on our side."

"I trust you," Laney said. "I'm ready to put this behind me."

Hearing her declaration of trust for all of them put Micah at ease. "You can come with me to meet him if you want."

"I really need to get to work. The Meyers are checking out today, and we have some new guests checking in. I want to meet him, but maybe some other time?" she offered.

"No problem." Micah reached over and laid a hand over hers. "I'll let him know what's going on. He goes to church with us, so we can have him over for lunch one Sunday."

Laney grinned. "That sounds perfect. Thank you so much." She leaned over and wrapped her arms around his neck.

"We've got this handled. You don't have to worry about Devin anymore."

Camille stood and said, "He's right. You're in good hands."

"I know," Laney said. "Thanks for all your help."

"Don't mention it," Haley said as she walked by. "I know how to erase that creep from your life. Just bring your phone to lunch."

Micah released Laney and waited for Camille and Haley to get back to work. "I'm going to pick you up a new phone today, if that's okay with you. I think a pre-pay phone would be safest."

"That sounds perfect. I really only need one so that your mom and Haley can get in touch with me. I hardly ever go far from the main house."

"Consider it done. I'll load it up so you'll be set for a while." He kissed her forehead and hugged her tight, lingering a few moments. "Why is it always so hard to leave you?" he whispered in her ear.

"I don't know, but I feel it too."

He leaned down and sealed his lips with hers. The gentle way she drew out the kiss was a testament to her patience. Laney needed a relationship that was lasting and constant, and he'd be the one to give her just that.

When they broke the kiss, Micah left his eyes closed. "I really have to go, but I don't want to."

"Same. Want to come over tonight?" she asked.

Knowing they wouldn't have anything to keep them from slipping into an endless string of kisses, Micah wasn't sure her offer was a good idea. He'd have to think of something to occupy their alone time if they'd be hanging out in the evenings.

With the idea to pick up a board game in town, he felt better about accepting her invitation. Surely the two feet of space the board provided was safe. "Sure. I'll let you know how things go with Asa today."

They reluctantly parted ways, and Micah texted Asa asking if he could meet for lunch. By the time he parked in front of the general store in Blackwater, Asa had texted back a time and place to meet.

Micah grabbed the burner phone, a game of Guess Who, and an alarm clock for Laney before picking up some household things he thought she would like. He left the store half an hour later with his arms loaded down with bags. He'd gotten a little carried away, but Laney would enjoy finding homes for the new things in her cabin. If she couldn't go to town alone, he'd bring the best he could to her.

Piling the bags in his truck, he made his way to Grady's Feed and Seed. Eyeing the bags of things he'd bought for Laney, he wondered how she'd made such a drastic change in his life in such a short time. He'd heard the saying, "When you know, you know," but he'd never put much stock in it. Turns out, he was wrong. He knew Laney was right for him. She'd changed his life for the better. He hadn't known he'd had more of himself to give until he wanted to give everything to Laney.

Grady stopped Micah in the feed store and inquired about everything from the spring calving to how Maddie's horse was doing since they'd added a supplement to her feed. The casual chatter kept his mind from slipping to Laney's ex and the payback he wanted to deliver. Surely Asa would have some good news.

Micah met Asa at The Basket Case for lunch. He rarely ate in town and usually stuck to something quick and easy, but they would have much more privacy here to talk.

Micah spotted Asa in a booth on the far side of the dining area and took the seat across from his friend.

Asa hadn't changed much since their high school days, but Micah knew how deceiving looks could be. The man had lost his wife in a car accident two years ago. Not only had they been high school sweethearts, she was also the mother of his child.

Losing someone that close to you had to change a man.

"Been a long time, friend." Micah greeted the officer with a handshake. The greeting was a joke. They saw each other every week at church.

"Too long. How's the family?" Asa asked.

Micah opened the menu and scanned the middle section. "Good. Yours?"

Asa linked his fingers and rested his arms on the table. "As good as we can be. Mom hasn't been the same since we lost Granny last year. She's still keeping Jacob while I work, but I think we might have to try something different soon. She's not taking it well."

"I hate that for your mom. I know they were close." Micah tried to swallow past his dry throat and wished someone would bring him a drink.

As if the mere thought had summoned her, a young girl with straight blonde hair stopped at their table.

"Hey, fellas. I'm Cindy. What can I get you today?" She poised a pen over the ordering pad and cocked her hip to one side.

"Water and the turkey on wheat, please," Asa said as he closed the menu.

Micah took one last glance at the menu before deciding. "Water and the classic cheeseburger."

"Got it." The waitress flashed a peppy smile and

turned on her heel with her blonde hair fanning behind her.

Asa sat back in his seat. "What can I do for you today?"

"It's about Laney."

"What about her?" Asa asked.

Micah had grown up with Asa, and the two had been as close as brothers. Laney wasn't the most outgoing member of the church yet, but everyone in town made a point to welcome a newcomer.

Micah rubbed the scruff on his chin. "She's got a problem with an ex."

Asa frowned. "I thought she was from out of town."

"Close to Cheyenne. You remember the shiner she had when she got here?" Micah asked.

"Oh yeah. It was hard to miss." Asa crossed his arms over his chest. The standard protective vest he wore beneath his uniform broadened his frame. "I tried asking her about it once, but she was pretty tight-lipped."

Their conversation halted as the waitress brought their drinks.

Micah waited until she was out of earshot to say, "Well, she told me when I first met her that it was her ex. She said she left him and her job back in Cheyenne. I found out last night that he's been calling and texting her since she left. Come to find out, it's almost nonstop. He called her back to back to back last night, and she said it's constant."

"Hmm. That's a red flag. Does he have a record?" Asa asked.

"Not that she mentioned. I don't know much about him, but I think with Laney's help we can piece together enough that you can check him out."

"Sure." Asa pulled a notepad and pen from his pocket. "Let's see what we can do right now. You can call me later and fill in the rest after you talk to Laney."

Their food arrived before they'd gotten through many questions, and they tied up the rest before moving on to lighter topics. Jacob was turning eight this month, and Asa had booked them a father-son fishing trip in Montana.

One thing Micah appreciated about his friend was the way he took care of his family and his job. They shared the same strong sense of responsibility. When their plates were clean, they didn't continue the idle chat.

Micah left The Basket Case feeling better about the situation with Laney's scumbag ex. He couldn't wait to get back and finish things up at the ranch so he could talk to Laney.

CHAPTER 17

LANEY

Laney sat next to Asa and his family in the decorated church. Everyone's attention was focused on the Harding family at the front as Noah and Camille vowed before their friends, family, and God to love, honor, and cherish one another for the rest of their lives.

Asa offered Laney a box of tissues, and she grabbed for it. She hadn't expected the flood of emotions being only a guest at a wedding. This was the first time she'd been witness to the beginning of a marriage, and her eyes tingled with the coming tears. Her friends, Noah and Camille, were perfect for each other.

Her attention drifted toward Micah standing tall beside his brothers, and the extent of the blessing she'd stumbled upon at Blackwater Ranch hit her square in the chest. She hadn't been sure she could trust him at first, but something had told her to open her heart to the ranch.

She thought about Asa and his son, Jacob, who had spent a few evenings at the ranch over the last week. They'd all chatted and gotten to know each other, but they'd also found time to talk about Laney's problems with her ex while Jacob played with Levi.

There were so many things she hadn't known about the man she'd lived with in Cheyenne. He had a criminal history of assault and a growing list of small claims lawsuits against him over the last decade. A familiar jolt of guilt filled her thoughts. She'd lived with a man who wasn't her husband, and she knew now what a mistake it had been. It was one of the first things she'd asked God to forgive when she learned how to pray.

Laney's attention was brought back to the present when the officiating pastor announced Noah and Camille as husband and wife, and the church filled with applause. Laney clapped and looked at Micah. He was looking back at her, and her heart swelled. He was the man God had meant for her. She knew it now as surely as she knew the forest green of his eyes. He was a man of few words, but she knew his heart by the selfless things he did daily, and she fell deeper in love with him every minute. Her heart moved closer to him every time he was near, begging to touch the one who had set her free from her old life.

Micah's gaze stayed fixed on Laney as the newly married couple made their way down the aisle and out the door of the church. Micah saw her when everyone else turned away. He saw more than the broken shell of a woman she'd been. He was filling her up, and her insides were screaming to thank him for waking her up to a life of happiness with him, the Hardings, and the Lord. This man was important to her. Her heart told her so every time he smiled at her.

The reception was held in the adjoining fellowship hall. Laney stayed close to Asa and his family while they waited for the wedding party to finish up some quick photos. After Asa's initial history check on Devin, the officer had been fairly certain her ex would give up. She hadn't heard from him since Micah had bought her the new phone, and it seemed Devin's connection had been severed.

When the wedding party entered the reception area to cheers and whistles, she spotted Micah at the same time he saw her. Everyone's mood seemed to be elevated with the joy of the celebration.

Micah reached her side, and his arms slid around her waist as he whispered in her ear, "You look beautiful."

She'd gone shopping with Camille earlier in the week, and Laney had found the beautiful hunter-green dress at a bargain outlet. She leaned into him and breathed in the spicy scent of sandalwood and leather. She'd never known Micah to wear cologne before now, and she closed her eyes as she tried to memorize the scent that tingled her nose.

Laney leaned back and rested her hands on his chest. "You clean up nice yourself."

Micah's suit was similar to the one he'd worn when they first met. They'd come a long way since that day.

Micah greeted Asa with a handshake. "I'm glad Laney had someone familiar to sit with today." Micah turned back to Laney. "Camille was upset she couldn't get you a bridesmaid dress in time."

Laney waved a hand. "Oh, I'm fine. I've never been in a wedding before, and I wouldn't know what to do. It was beautiful, and I'm glad I got to watch."

Micah stayed by her side for the rest of the evening. The dinner was amazing, and the air was filled with laughter. After the meal was cleared, everyone watched as the lights dimmed and Noah and Camille shared their first dance as husband and wife. The song ended, and the father-daughter dance began. Laney swallowed the longing in her throat as Camille rested her head on the shoulder of a gray-haired man.

Mama Harding and Noah joined the dance toward the end, and Laney brushed a single tear from her cheek. What a blessing that her friends had loving families to share this day with them.

Micah leaned closer to Laney until his cheek brushed against hers. Her skin tingled at the slight touch, and her ear hummed as his deep voice whispered, "Do you want to dance?"

She turned slightly to look into his eyes. "Yes." The word was barely audible, but she was still reeling from Micah's attention. Love filled the atmosphere, and she felt as light as air. She might be floating on cloud nine. She'd heard that expression, and this must be what it felt like.

She followed Micah to the area that had been cleared for dancing. He pulled her close, and she rested her head against his chest. Haley caught Laney's attention across the room and gave a big two thumbs up with some dramatic eyebrow dancing. She turned her face to Micah's chest to keep from laughing at her friend.

They danced through two more slow songs before the fast beat of a pop song had them both shaking their heads. Thankfully, they were on the same page, and a few slow dances seemed to be their shared limit.

When they sat down at a white-linen-covered table, Micah pulled his phone from his pocket. "Good grief. Jameson called me three times." He pressed the button to return the call and immediately began talking.

"What's up?" Micah stared at Laney's hand that he held in his while he listened to Jameson. A few seconds later, he huffed a sigh. "Got it. I'll bring Aaron with me. We'll be there in about ten, but we need to change first. Give us twenty."

Micah removed the phone from his ear and turned to Laney. "The bull broke through the fence. Half the herd is out."

"Go," Laney said, urging him toward the exit.

"Are you sure? I hate to run, but—"

Laney held up a hand. "Go find Aaron. I'll be fine. I can ride home with Asher and Haley."

The indecision on Micah's face had her reaching to place a gentle hand on his cheek. "I'm really fine. I know you need to go. Let me know if I can do anything from here. If you get there and find out you need more hands, call me and tell me who to send."

Micah leaned in and kissed her forehead. "I'll call you when I can."

She watched him dodge through the crowd of people toward his brother. The last thing she wanted to do was keep him from taking care of the ranch and the people who lived there. One day he would realize they were in this together.

"Hey." Haley plopped down in the seat Micah vacated. Her shining auburn hair was swept back in a bustle of perfect curls. "What's up with Micah?"

"Jameson called and said a fence was down and half the herd was out."

"Are you serious?" She stood. "I'll get Asher."

"Are you sure? He's taking Aaron with him. I told him to call me if he needed more help."

Haley turned from her husband to Laney and back. "Well, I'm just thinking maybe they could get them rounded up faster with more hands."

Laney pointed toward Asher. "He's having fun. What about Hunter?"

They scanned the room until they spotted him at the same time. Sure enough, Hunter was leaning back in a chair on the far side of the room. His arms were crossed over his chest, and he looked as if he'd rather be anywhere but here.

"Just the man we need." Haley strode to him and explained the situation. Laney couldn't hear the conversation from this distance, but Haley's hand gestures were dramatic enough to be telling the story of a catastrophic natural disaster instead of a few stray cattle.

Hunter stood and walked off, leaving Haley mid-sentence. With Hunter on his way, Haley gave Laney a conspiratorial wink. Her drawn-out story had probably pushed Hunter out the door quicker.

With Micah gone, Laney moved around the room talking with the townspeople she was getting to know. Everyone had welcomed her here, and she felt at ease in every conversation, even without one of the Hardings by her side.

An hour later, Haley appeared at Laney's side. "Hey, you riding with us? We're taking the gifts back to the ranch, so we thought we'd get a head start."

"Sure. I'll help." Laney tossed her punch cup in the trash and loaded her arms with beautifully wrapped gifts. Once they'd loaded Asher's truck, they started back to the ranch.

Asher left the light on in the cab as he drove, and Haley kept a firm grip on his hand. Laney had heard about Haley's fear of the dark, but she'd almost forgotten. Haley had quickly jumped into the truck, but other than that, she seemed to be holding up. She talked the entire way back to the ranch. Maybe the conversation kept her mind from focusing on her fear.

Micah's truck was parked at the main house, and Laney asked to be dropped off there. The echoing thud of her heels against the wooden floor was loud in the empty meeting room. After checking all the common areas, she found him in the small office at the back of the house.

His head rested in his hands, but he looked up when she stopped in the doorway.

"Hey." His tired voice reflected the exhaustion in his eyes.

He'd changed out of his wedding suit into camouflage pants and a dark-gray thermal shirt. She loved the way the material stretched over his thick shoulders and chest, not to mention his arms. Micah was built for the hard work the ranch required. They'd all been up since dawn rushing around before the wedding, and Laney's eyelids were getting heavy.

"Hey. Is everything okay?" she asked. She held her breath as she waited for his response.

When things had gone wrong at the bar, Devin had taken his frustrations out on Laney. She knew to stay as far from him as possible when he was in a foul mood. He'd throw a long string of curses at her. If he could get his hands on her, he'd grab her shoulders to shake the good sense out of her before shoving her to the floor.

Micah rubbed both hands over his face and sighed. When he turned to her, his eyes were bloodshot. "We got them all back in. I left Hunter and Jameson to mend the fence." His face was void of expression as he turned to the computer. "I'm too old to be running after cattle, and I despise bookkeeping."

Laney twisted her finger. She'd never been good at saying the right thing at the right time. "I'm sorry."

Micah looked at her and shoved his chair away from the computer. "Come here."

She stepped into the small office and sat on Micah's leg. His arms wrapped around her, and he rested his head on her shoulder with a sigh. His hug was tight and gentle, and as she wrapped her arms around him, she felt the tension leave his tight muscles.

"Much better," he whispered.

She leaned her cheek against his head, knowing Micah was different. Even on his bad days, he was good to her. Settled in his arms, she knew he needed her as much as she needed him, and she would spend an endless number of days devoted to easing his burdens.

Laney looked at the spreadsheet on the computer. "Is there anything I can help with? I used to do the bookkeeping for the bar." She turned to Micah with a knowing grin. "Maybe that's why he kept bugging me to come back."

Micah squeezed her tighter. "Way too soon to be joking about him. I still want to ram my fist into his face for what he did to you."

Laney brushed a hand over his hair. "It's over. I've been praying about it, and I'm ready to put it behind me. I'm not sure how to forgive him like I'm supposed to, but maybe one day I can."

Micah lifted his head, and his gaze fell over every inch of her face. From her hair to her jaw, Micah studied her with an intensity she'd never known, but she didn't want to hide from him.

"You're so good," he whispered as the pad of his

thumb brushed across the cheek where her bruise had once been.

He was good. When others saw his gruff and stern demeanor, she knew it was his determination and honor. He stood by his word and never hesitated to lend a hand when someone was in need. He worked long hours on the ranch in the rain and snow only to come inside and do more work.

His hand slid to the back of her neck, and his gaze dropped to her lips. Without hesitation, she leaned into him, wordlessly sealing the bond between them. His hand splayed on her back against the thin material of her dress, the heat of his skin seeping into hers and radiating throughout her body. Her hand rested on his jaw before sliding to his neck.

Micah pulled away, breathing hard and resting as far back against his seat as possible.

"What's wrong?" Laney asked.

He rubbed a hand over his chin. "Nothing. You're just too much to take in tonight."

"Tired of me?" she joked.

"No, it's the opposite. There's no one else for me. You're it."

Laney's breath stopped in her throat. Words wouldn't go out and air wouldn't go in.

Micah saved her the embarrassment of fumbling her words. "I need to get back to work. You want me to drop you off at your place first?"

"Um, no. If it's okay with you, I'll just read in the living room." She didn't want to leave him tonight. There had been a shift between them, and she was afraid it would disappear if they separated now. It was silly, but she was desperate to cling to the comfort she found when he was near.

Exhaustion weighed on him, and he sighed. "I don't want to get back to work."

Laney smiled at the realization that he was feeling the same connection she was. She stood and adjusted her dress. It was the nicest piece of clothing she'd ever owned, and she wasn't ready to change into pajamas just yet anyway. "Let me know when you're ready to go."

He reached for her hand as she turned to leave. "Wait. Would you really be able to help me with this?" He gestured to the computer. "I'd love to hand this part of the business over to someone else, and you probably know more about this stuff than I do."

The level of trust necessary to allow her to step into a role that handled the finances of the ranch that supported his entire family wasn't lost on her. "Sure."

"We can sit down and go over everything one day next week if you want. It would come with a raise, of course."

"Okay. Thank you." It was hard to push the words out without choking on her emotions.

He released her hand and his mouth quirked up in a tired smile. "I won't be long."

She slipped out of the room and stood in the hallway with a hand over her heart. Micah was letting her into his life and opening his home to her where they could work together to build something for their future, and Laney would stand beside him through it all.

CHAPTER 18
LANEY

After spending so much time talking with everyone at the wedding, Laney felt like a part of the church. Everyone greeted her by name now, and they went out of their way to see how she was doing. She was putting names with faces and trying to remember who was related to whom.

She loved being at church every Sunday. She looked forward to it. The caring community was like an extension of the Harding family's acceptance. She'd been welcomed in with open arms.

She wasn't an outsider. For the first time in her life, she felt like she was a part of something bigger than herself. Sitting amongst the Harding family, she felt like one of them.

Micah squeezed her hand and whispered, "Hey, you okay?"

Laney nodded. She was okay. She was great,

excellent, fantastic. But the stirring in her heart was new. She hadn't decided if it was nerves or eagerness. It was something unknown, and she kept circling the feeling that had her awareness piqued. What was it?

Linda, the worship leader, introduced Asher and Haley who would be singing a duet. Laney had heard her friends sing many times now, and they made the perfect pair. She got lost in the song, opening her heart to the lyrics and music.

That foreign inkling in her middle was growing. It was almost like an urgency, but for what?

The pastor took his place behind the podium and thanked Asher and Haley for sharing their beautiful gifts. Laney squeezed Haley's hand as she took the seat beside her.

"Please open your Bibles to Matthew chapter five."

"Oh," Haley whispered, "The Beatitudes. This is my favorite."

Laney flipped through her Bible looking for the book of Matthew. She still wasn't very good at finding things. The Bible was huge. "What are Beatitudes?" she asked.

Haley's friendly grin widened. "Blessings."

Oh, that cleared things up. Laney knew all about blessings. She'd experienced one after the other since coming to Blackwater.

Brother Higgins led a prayer that the Lord would

show them the meaning of His word this morning. Laney appreciated the prayer. At least she wasn't the only one praying for understanding.

Throughout the service, Laney listened as Brother Higgins recounted the Beatitudes and the promises of the Heavenly Father. She found herself inching to the edge of her seat as he spoke.

Blessed are the meek, for they shall inherit the earth.

Blessed are those who hunger and thirst for right-eousness, for they shall be satisfied.

Blessed are the peacemakers, for they shall be called sons of God.

Rejoice and be glad, for your reward is great in heaven.

Your reward? Heaven? She wanted that. That was the blessing—salvation.

She kept her seat until the end of the service, and the pianist played a soft hymn asking all who were tired and lost to come home.

Home. She wanted that too.

If she wanted it, she'd have to take it for herself. She'd have to open her heart completely to Christ, and she was ready.

Micah rested his hand on hers, and she turned to him. His expression was questioning.

She whispered, "I want to go."

Micah nodded with understanding. "I'll go with you."

She kept her hold on his hand as they moved out

of the aisle. Everyone was looking at them, but she didn't care. She was on a mission, and Micah was by her side.

They approached the altar, and Laney looked down at the few steps. This was it. She felt Micah's quiet strength on one side and the presence of the Lord on the other.

She knelt on the bottom step and bowed her head. Seconds later, she felt a firm hand on her shoulder, and she knew it was Brother Higgins.

She sucked in a shaky breath and whispered, "God, I'm sorry. I've made a mess of things, but I don't want to be that person anymore. I want to follow You and live for You. I want to know You. I know You're my Savior. Amen."

Brother Higgins whispered a prayer and assurances to her. He asked her questions, and she answered them. She did want to be a Christian. She did want to follow Christ.

She lifted her head and wiped the moisture from her eyes. Her heart felt heavy, but in a good way. It was filled with something new and hopeful.

Looking around, she saw that the entire Harding family knelt around her. They filled the front of the small church, supporting her as she made the biggest decision of her life.

Then there was Micah, kneeling before the Father. His head was bowed in prayer for her, and the floodgates of her heart were opened to him. A man who would pray for her salvation, her healing, and her saving grace was a man to be cherished. He was the man she needed in her life, and this was the family she desperately wanted to call her own.

Laney swallowed the lump in her throat as Micah lifted his head. She flung her arms around his neck and tucked her face into his shoulder. She'd spent her entire life alone because she hadn't opened her heart to Christ. Now, He would always be with her, and she would never be alone again.

The life she had lived until today was gone. Here and now, she wanted a new life with this family surrounding her. A new life with Christ in her heart.

CHAPTER 19
MICAH

Saturdays were the busiest for Laney and the bed and breakfast. Micah had witnessed the change in Laney's confidence and the overall way she held herself since she went to the altar last week. He'd started spending evenings at her cabin, and she often asked questions about things she'd marked in her Bible or a devotional. She was practically glowing with happiness.

Micah leaned against the wall in the meeting room next to his brother, Aaron, while Laney welcomed the newest guest. She gestured to various places throughout the large room.

The guest was a tall man with styled hair who wore slacks and a white button-up shirt. The man hadn't turned his attention to any of the places or things Laney indicated. His gaze had only left her once to check his phone.

"Uncle Micah!" Levi yelled.

Micah pried his attention from the new guest. "What's up, bud?"

"Can I stay with Laney today?"

Micah snuck a glance at Laney and the man who had moved closer to her in the seconds Levi had been talking. "I think she's busy today. Lots of guests are checking in and out."

Levi tilted his head. "What about Maddie?"

"That sounds like a good idea. She'll need a hand getting the horses ready for tomorrow. I think one of the couples coming in wanted to ride in the morning."

"Okay!" Levi shouted over his shoulder as he ran off to find Maddie.

Micah wanted to catch Laney's attention before he left for town, but it seemed like she was tied up for a while. The man's attention was still locked on Laney as she spoke.

Micah's mother caught his attention from the serving bar and waved him over. "Are you going to town?"

"Headed there now. You need something?"

"Laundry detergent. I don't know how I missed it on my list, but we're all out."

"Sure. Anything else?"

"That's all. Thanks."

He leaned in and wrapped one arm around her shoulder. "Anytime."

He caught another glance at Laney and the new guest who typed something on his phone and shoved it back into his pocket before turning back to Laney with an interested stare.

She wasn't flirting, but the man was clearly attracted to her. Micah knew Laney was good at her job, and that required a friendly welcome. She looked up just as he was leaving and waved.

Micah waved back and headed for town. If he could speed through his errands, he could get back to the ranch early for supper.

He'd just walked into Grady's when his phone rang. It was Asa, and Micah answered as he made his way to the dog food section.

"Hey."

"You got a minute?" Asa asked. His tone was all business.

"Sure."

"Is Laney around?"

Micah stopped, no longer seeing the piled bags of dog food. "No. Why?"

"I had an alert on Laney's name. One showed up this morning that might be her."

"What's the alert for?" Micah asked.

"A man named Colton Erwin filed a police report in Laramie County. He claims an employee named Laney Parker embezzled thousands of dollars from his establishment."

Micah rubbed his chin, completely distracted

from his errand. "Erwin. That's her ex's last name. Is it the same bar?"

"It is. The business is registered to both of them. They're brothers."

"She hasn't mentioned Devin's brother. Embezzlement? That doesn't sound like Laney."

"You're right," Asa agreed. "But it could explain why she left Cheyenne so suddenly. Maybe they were on to her."

"You can't be serious. This is Laney," Micah said.

"I know. I don't know what to think of it either. Laney doesn't seem like a con."

Micah rubbed a hand over his brow. "Let me talk to her. I just asked her to take over the bookkeeping for the ranch last week."

"Yikes," Asa said. "Was that her idea or yours?"

"Mine. She mentioned she handled the finances for the bar."

Asa sighed. "I don't want to falsely accuse, and she's innocent until proven guilty."

"This just doesn't look good. I really don't think she would do something like that."

"Me either. We just need to figure out what this means."

"What *could* it mean for her?" Micah asked.

"I don't know yet, and I don't want to say anything until I know."

"Okay. I'll talk to her."

"Stay alert. If she's a master manipulator, she's fooled us all."

Micah's chest felt heavy. Could he have fallen for a woman who was manipulating him into getting her hands on the ranch's finances? "I'll let you know."

He disconnected the call with Asa and called Laney.

She answered on the second ring. "Hello."

"Hey. Where are you?" Micah tried to keep the tension from his voice, but he was sure someone had wrapped a barbed wire around his throat.

"On my way to town with Maddie and Levi."

Micah could hear Levi talking in the background. "Okay. Can you meet me at Grady's and ride home with me?" He wasn't sure if he could work up the nerve to question her on the way home, but at least he could gauge her actions. If he could just be with her, he'd be reassured of her innocence.

"Sure. We're actually on our way to Grady's now. We didn't know you were there."

"Okay. See you in a few." He ended the call quickly and paced the aisle. Laney wasn't a thief. He was certain of it.

"Micah?"

He looked up to see Olivia Lawrence walking toward him with a bubbly smile on her face.

"What a surprise," she said with her usual enthusiasm. "It's good to see you."

"You too." He was too focused on the accusation against Laney to temper his gruff response.

"How's the family?" she asked.

He didn't have the time or patience for idle conversation with Olivia right now. His thoughts were swirling around Laney and the embezzlement accusation.

Olivia's phone rang in the pocket of her coat. "Oh, I'm sorry. Let me grab that."

Micah tried to motion that he would talk to her another time, but her eyes widened and he knew something was wrong.

"What?" Her hand rose to her mouth. "Are you serious?" She paused and nodded as if the person on the other end of the call could see her affirmation. "I'm on my way." She cradled the phone in her hands and stared at it.

"Is everything okay?" he asked, praying she would say it was nothing.

"It's Mom. She had a heart attack. The paramedics are with her now, and they're taking her to Cody." Olivia's expression crumbled, and tears streamed down her face. "Mom!"

Micah had no idea how to calm her down, but her reaction was spiraling into panic. "What can I do?" When in doubt, ask.

"I need to get to her." Olivia sucked in ragged breaths that bordered on hysteria.

Olivia and her mom had always been close. They

were more like best friends than anything. Growing up with only brothers, she'd clung to her mother.

"You can't go like this." He looked around for anyone who could help. "I'll drive you."

Olivia nodded and continued sobbing into her hand.

Looks like his errands for the day were sidetracked. He needed to get Olivia to the hospital, and he could get the things they needed in town later.

Olivia wailed as he closed the passenger door of his truck with her inside. He sent a quick text to Laney. Putting off talking to her meant he would have to wait for answers. He was the worst at comforting others, and Cody felt way too far to ride with a hysterical passenger.

CHAPTER 20

LANEY

Laney looked around Grady's enormous warehouse. "Where do you think he'd be?"

Maddie scanned the store. "Not sure. We can ask Grady if we run into him."

"Dog food!" Levi guessed.

Laney squeezed the kid's hand and followed Maddie to the horse feed section. She pointed out the feed they'd be getting, and Levi asked a series of unending questions. He knew so much about farming for a four-year-old, and she assumed it was because he listened to everything.

When they'd gathered everything they needed, Laney checked her phone. "Still no word from Micah."

"Oh, well. Looks like you get to stick with us," Maddie said.

They found Grady on their way to checkout with

the pallet of horse feed, and the older man approached them with open arms.

"Come here boy! You're growing like a weed."

Levi ran into Grady's arms. They could have passed for a grandpa and grandson.

Grady sat Levi back on his feet. "We need a big rock to put on your head so you stop growing."

"No way. I'm gonna be as big as Daddy," Levi said.

Grady stood and propped his hands on his hips. "Oh, I believe that. The Harding boys are big and strong."

"Yep. I'm gonna be big and strong too."

"Good boy," Grady said as he turned to the pallet of feed Maddie was pushing on a flat cart. "The horses send you today?"

Maddie propped on the handle of the cart. "You know it. Those beasts keep me running." She tilted her head to Laney. "Lucas is working at the fire station today, so Laney is my helper."

"And me!" Levi cried.

"And you, of course," Maddie added.

Grady jerked a thumb over his shoulder. "You just missed Micah. I saw him run out of here with Olivia just a minute ago."

Laney stood paralyzed at the mention of Olivia Lawrence. The beautiful woman from the neighboring farm definitely had her sights set on Micah.

"Olivia?" Maddie said. "They left together?"

Laney fought to keep her feet from stepping backward. She didn't want to hear about Micah leaving with Olivia when he'd asked her to meet him here only minutes ago.

"Yeah. They looked like they were in a hurry," Grady said.

Had Micah run into Olivia and ran from the store hoping to dodge Laney? It didn't make sense. He'd been in town running errands for the ranch. At least, that's what he'd said he would be doing today. Now, he was with Olivia. Laney twisted her finger and glanced from one side to the other, desperate to run from this conversation.

"Well, that's strange. I wonder what the rush was about," Maddie asked.

"Beats me. I've got to run. Have a good one." Grady turned to Levi. "And you stay out of trouble."

"I will!" Levi assured.

They paid for the horse feed without talking about Micah and Olivia. Levi continued to chatter, unaware of Laney's mounting insecurities.

Micah had promised her commitment and loyalty, and she had believed him. She'd been so sure of their relationship just this morning. Now, all she could think about was him running off with Olivia.

Once everyone was settled in Maddie's truck, she turned to Laney. "Why don't you give him a call?

See if everything is okay and if he wants us to take care of the stuff in town today."

Laney nodded. "Okay. Right. That's a good idea." Her thoughts had been too jumbled to think of calling him. But as she pressed the button to call him, she wondered if he would ignore her call because he was with Olivia and didn't want Laney to know.

When the call went unanswered, Laney's hope sank further.

"I'm sure he's just busy. He'll call back when he gets a chance," Maddie said as they merged back into the road leading out of town.

Levi carried the conversation on the way back to the ranch. Laney and Maddie only spoke to answer his questions. If Maddie was concerned about Micah's disappearance with Olivia, Laney knew she had good reason to worry as well.

When they parked in front of the main house at the ranch, Laney grabbed the door, prepared to jump out. She looked out at the wide-open fields past the house and wanted to run until her body couldn't take it anymore.

"Laney," Maddie said.

Laney turned to her friend, but her skin was tingling with the urge to get out of the truck.

"I don't think Micah meant to ditch you. If he left with Olivia, there's a reason. Micah isn't a two-timer."

Laney could hear the sincerity in Maddie's words, and she knew they were true herself. It was hard to push her worries and doubts aside and remember that Micah hadn't given her any reason not to trust him.

He had trusted her on word alone when she was a stranger. He deserved the benefit of the doubt, and she took the first easy breath since they spoke to Grady. "You're right. I know that. I'm sure it was just something that came up."

Maddie squeezed Laney's shoulder. "I trust him."

Laney nodded. "I do too." She really did, and saying the words aloud made them stronger. "Thank you. I feel silly for even thinking—"

Maddie cut her off. "It is silly. Micah would never do that to you. He cares about you, and anyone with eyes can see it. You'll hear from him soon."

A rush of appreciation filled Laney's heart. She'd never had someone to look out for her the way the Hardings did.

Maddie wasn't a Harding yet, but she was just like the rest, and they didn't deceive people.

"Thanks again. I feel better," Laney said as she grabbed the door handle once more.

"Anytime." Maddie returned her hands to the wheel as if the matter was settled.

Laney waved a quick good-bye to Levi and

jumped from the truck. She'd settled in the new guests around lunch, and now it was time to help Mama Harding get supper ready.

She stepped into the warm meeting room and hung her jacket on the hook by the door. The room was empty save for a man sitting at one of the tables near the stairs. He lifted his head at her entrance and stood.

"Hey. I was hoping to see you again." It was one of the new guests, Brett Caldwell. He'd kept her talking until way after lunch, and she didn't have time to stop and chat.

"Hey. I was just about to help with supper." She was still coming down from the roller coaster of emotions she'd experienced on the drive back from town, and she wasn't in the mood to talk.

He met her near the door leading to the kitchen and stood too close for her liking.

"I was just wondering if you'd like to take a walk with me. I'd like to see the ranch." His stare was intent on her, almost daring her to deny him.

"Um, I really need to get back to work. Maybe one of the men can show you around tomorrow."

His expression fell at her suggestion. "I was really hoping to spend the time with you."

Laney linked her hands, trying to refrain from nervously twisting her finger. "I'm sorry. I don't know if I mentioned it earlier, but I'm seeing someone. Micah, the ranch manager, is my boyfriend."

"Oh, well, we could still take a walk as friends," he said, undeterred by her confession.

"Well, I'm not sure that would be appropriate. And I'm on the clock now."

"What time do you get off?" he asked.

His relentlessness had a pit of unease growing in Laney's middle. "Well after dark. It's not a good idea to be out on the ranch at night, even if you're armed." Micah and his brothers had told her as much, and she'd always appreciated Micah's willingness to drive her home each evening.

"Okay, you just let me know when you're free."

Laney warred with her duty to be friendly to the guest and the uneasy feeling the man was giving her. She wasn't comfortable being alone with him, and she stepped toward the kitchen.

Just as Laney reached for the knob, the door swung open.

"There you are," Mama Harding said. "Can you give me a hand?"

"Yes," Laney quickly said. "I was just on my way to find you."

Mama Harding turned to Brett with a smile. "Hi Mr. Caldwell. Can I help you with anything?"

"Oh no. I was just going back to my room."

Laney studied him, wondering if he'd intentionally left out his pursuit of alone time with her.

"You know, Maddie can show you around at the stables if you like horses," Mama Harding said.

Laney prayed he'd decline the offer. She had a bad feeling about this guy, and it went deeper than his persistence. She didn't like the idea of him being in the stables alone with Maddie and Levi.

"Nah. I think I'll get some work done." He waved a hand as he turned to the stairs.

Laney breathed a sigh of relief and hurried into the kitchen with Mama Harding. Laney threw her energy into the meal prep, hoping to forget about the lack of communication from Micah and the stranger's advances. She wanted to call Micah again, but she also didn't want to come across as needy. When she hadn't heard from him when supper was ready an hour later, her worry began anew.

As they placed the last side dish on the serving counter, Laney scanned the faces in the meeting room looking for Micah. Her attention stalled on Aaron who held his cell to his ear.

"What? When did this happen?" he asked the person on the other side of the call. His chin rose, and his gaze landed on his mother. "We'll be there in a few."

Raising his hand, he whistled to gain everyone's attention. "Listen up. Micah just called. Martha Lawrence had a heart attack today, and she didn't make it."

Mama Harding's hands covered a pained gasp. "Oh, Martha."

Laney had heard Mama Harding talk about the

neighbor woman. They'd been friends since grade school and often helped each other out. Laney folded her hands in front of her mouth. Mama Harding had lost one of her best friends today, and that meant Olivia lost her mother.

Maddie rushed to Mama Harding's side and helped her sit in a nearby chair. Guests crowded close to the Harding family with condolences, but Laney's attention had stopped on Brett who typed relentlessly on his phone, unfazed by the grief that had just washed over the household.

Mama Harding succumbed to her tears, and Silas knelt next to her, letting her cry on his shoulder.

Remorse sat heavy on Laney's shoulders as everyone tried to process the news. The family needed time to grieve, and she could step up and help as much as possible to give them time with each other.

Laney gestured for the bed and breakfast guests. "Go ahead and help yourselves." The Hardings seemed to have lost their appetites, so she moved the remaining food to storage bowls in the kitchen.

She was just putting the last of the food away when Mama Harding entered the kitchen.

"Hey, what can I do to help?" Laney asked, knowing Mama Harding would want things to continue to run at the ranch, but she might not feel up to doing it herself.

"Did you make yourself a plate?" Mama Harding asked with tired eyes.

"No. I'll just get a sandwich later."

Mama Harding looked at the leftovers. "I'd like to take this to Jerry Lawrence. I don't want them worrying about meals right now."

"That's a good idea. You want me to grab one of the frozen dinners too?" Mama Harding kept a stash of pre-prepared meals in the event she wasn't able to cook.

"Yes. That would be nice. Thank you, Laney."

"You're welcome. I'm happy to help with anything."

Mama Harding opened her arms to Laney, and she stepped into the embrace. They didn't speak as the older woman drew comfort from Laney's strength. The Hardings had done so much for her these last few months, and she was more than willing to provide a shoulder for Mama Harding to cry on.

Laney stepped back. "I'll grab some things from the freezer."

Mama Harding wiped her eyes. "Thanks."

Laney gathered and bagged the food, and Aaron and Silas carried it to their trucks.

"I'll stay here in case the guests need anything. You can all go and be with your friends," Laney said.

Mama Harding reached for Laney's hand, her expression one of gratefulness and sadness. "I don't know what we would do without you, Laney. Thank you."

"Go on. I'll take care of things," Laney assured her.

All of the ranch workers left for the Lawrence farm, and Laney returned to the meeting room to check on the guests who were just finishing their meal. Everyone expressed condolences for the family's loss before settling into their rooms for the evening.

Laney finished cleaning up the meeting room and kitchen, taking her time to make sure everything would be back in working order when Mama Harding returned. The sadness on the matriarch's face tonight would haunt Laney's dreams. She didn't know the heartbreak of death, and after seeing the sadness amongst the Hardings, she wouldn't wish it on her worst enemy.

The house was uncharacteristically quiet without the voices of the family filling its walls. Micah gave her a ride to the main house this morning, and while her cabin wasn't far, she knew better than to venture out on the ranch alone. The Hardings had told her horror stories of their encounters with wildlife on the ranch, and she'd rather not come face-to-face with a mountain lion unarmed.

She pulled her phone from her back pocket and saw a missed call from Micah. He'd called hours ago, and she'd missed it. She'd been so busy taking care of things for the Hardings that she hadn't noticed or heard the ring.

He hadn't been sneaking off with another woman. He was helping a friend through a terrible time, and his willingness to drop everything for someone in need completely changed her perspective on the situation. She'd been right to trust him, and she felt guilty for doubting him at all today.

After spending most of her waking hours surrounded by the family and guests, the silence pricked her skin. She'd grown used to having people near to talk to at any moment.

Remembering her old friend, she decided to sit outside and talk to Dixie. She'd catch a ride back to her cabin with the first person who came home.

She grabbed her coat off the rack and stepped out onto the porch. She squinted, trying to see past the glow of the porch lights. "Dixie," she called as she crossed her arms over her chest. Laney turned to the left and right, listening for the dog. She usually stayed close to the main house around mealtimes hoping to catch some scraps from Levi. The kid snuck food into his pockets for Dixie every day.

Laney sat on the top step of the porch and waited. She missed Micah. Not because she hadn't seen him since lunch, but because she felt like she owed him an apology, even if he would never know she'd doubted his loyalty today.

Dixie came running around the porch and slowed as she neared Laney on the steps.

"Hey, girl. Long time no see." Laney had been working longer hours and spending less time at her cabin alone with the dog lately. Her relationship with the Hardings was growing stronger, and she wanted to spend every minute she could with them. They were the family she'd always hoped for as a little girl.

Laney scratched Dixie's neck. "You keeping the men in line? Do they listen to you? You're a smart girl." Leaning her forehead against the dog's, Laney closed her eyes and thanked God for leading her here.

The door opened behind her, and she turned to see Brett Caldwell closing the door behind him. She didn't want to be alone, but she also didn't have the energy to put on her best welcoming face.

"What are you doing out here alone?" he asked as he crossed his arms over his chest.

"Nothing. Just spending some time with Dixie." Laney reached for the dog, but Dixie had moved to her other side, tense and focused on Brett.

"It's okay, girl. He's a guest." Laney looked back at Brett. "Sorry. She's not used to having all the new faces around here."

Brett stared out into the dark beyond the porch. "It's fine."

Laney stood and dusted off her jeans. "You need

anything?" she asked.

"No. Just seeing what you were up to." He pulled his phone from his pocket and checked the screen before shoving it away.

She put her back against the wooden column framing the porch entrance and looked around for something to talk about. "Where did you say you're from?" she asked.

Brett's gaze scanned the darkness. "South. Not far."

"Oh." The quality of conversation wasn't off to a stellar start. "What brings you here?" A flash of light caught her eye as a vehicle drew closer down the long drive.

"Work."

Brett hadn't mentioned what he did for a living, and Laney thought the question was too personal to ask. If he'd wanted to share, he would have. "Well, looks like someone made it back from the Lawrences."

Brett stayed quiet beside her. He didn't seem too happy at the idea of the Hardings returning. His conversation had been tense and strained this evening. Was something bothering him? Had she done something that would lead him to post a bad review on a travel site?

Relief filled her chest as the vehicle parked nearby, but her relief was replaced by ice in her blood as she recognized the truck.

Laney had sidestepped the column at her back and was retreating before Devin stepped from the truck. She turned to Brett to find his attention locked on her as if he were a predator gauging the movements of his prey.

Work. Brett was here to find Laney—for Devin. And she'd foolishly told him anything he'd asked about her. She'd led Devin right to her door.

In a flash of movement, Brett lunged for her, grabbing her arm as she tried to dart away from him. With a jerk, she was thrown into his chest, and his strong arms restrained her instantly. Panic gripped her as she thrashed against him. He was too strong. The fight was over before it began.

Dixie growled and barked as Laney continued to jerk in Brett's arms. It was doing little good, but she was determined to go down swinging.

"Laney, stop and listen! You have to come back. I need you." Devin's authoritative order commanded her obedience.

Before, she would have stilled and bent to his will. Now, she had too much to lose, and she'd never cower to anyone again.

When she continued to strain against her bonds, Devin grabbed her shoulders. "I said stop it!"

"No! Get away from me!" Laney yelled. Rage fueled her, burning her from the inside as she kicked at him.

The back of his hand stung against her face, and

she panted in her anger. Tingles remained in the seconds after impact.

"I said stop!" Devin yelled.

Dixie growled and lunged for his leg, but he kicked her away with his boot.

Laney gasped as Dixie whined and bolted just out of reach.

A beam of headlights shone on the front of the main house as another vehicle approached.

When Brett and Devin turned toward the beams, Laney renewed her efforts to escape from Brett's restraint. If they had another man coming to help, her only chance to escape was now.

"Get her in the truck," Devin ordered.

"No! No!"

Laney thrashed, and Brett's grip tightened, bruising her arms. She pushed and bent as far as possible, but Brett's grip held firm as he dragged her toward Devin's truck. If she screamed loud enough, maybe one of the guests would hear.

"Shut up!" Brett yelled in her ear as his arm curled around her neck.

The headlights were blinding as she gasped for breath. At least she hoped the bright lights were headlights. Stars and flashes replaced everything else in her vision until she wasn't sure which way was up.

The burning fire within her dimmed to nothing more than an ember as darkness engulfed the light.

CHAPTER 21
MICAH

Micah leaned his head back against the seat in his truck. The headlights illuminated the familiar road home. Thankfully, he knew this stretch of asphalt like the back of his hand. His eyelids were getting heavy, and it was barely eight in the evening.

He'd been consumed by the Lawrence family's tragedy. Feeling useless and in the way, he'd left the grieving neighbors when the rest of his family showed up.

His phone rang in the cup holder beside him, and his friend's name lit up on the screen.

Micah answered. "Hey, man. Sorry I haven't gotten back to you."

"No problem. I heard about Martha Lawrence," Asa said.

"Yeah, she was a good woman." Martha and her family had helped the Hardings out more times than he could count. Micah always thought of her as part of his extended family, like an aunt. "I'm just leaving their place."

"No news on Laney?" Asa asked.

Micah turned by the Blackwater Ranch sign. "No, and I have no idea what to do. It's Laney! I don't believe she would do something like that."

"The more I think about it, the more I agree with you. It doesn't make sense."

Micah sighed. "I'll tell her what you told me, and we'll figure out what's going on."

"Let me know if I can help. If she can point us in the right direction, we might be able to piece together what this guy is up to."

"I'm almost there." He didn't like the idea of Laney being alone at the main house. She wasn't all alone, since the guests were there. Haley was close, since she took Levi home to put him to bed.

Still, Laney didn't like being alone, and he didn't like leaving her to feel that way. She might have been handling things on her own before she came here, but that wasn't the case anymore.

"Let me know," Asa said.

"Wait." Micah leaned over the steering wheel as his headlights fell on three people in front of the main house. One smaller person was being dragged quickly toward a truck while the other two crowded close. "Something's up."

"Like what?"

Micah leaned on the accelerator. "It's Laney. Someone has her."

"I'm on my way." Asa disconnected the call.

Micah tossed the phone into the passenger seat. Heat filled his body despite the chill in the night air. He tightened his grip on the steering wheel and slammed on the brakes. Someone had a death wish, and Micah was ready for battle.

No one laid a hand on Laney and got away with it.

He slung the truck into park and didn't bother killing the engine. He jumped out and ran toward the area just beyond the porch lit up by the headlights.

Someone was pushing Laney into the back seat of his truck in a rush, and when the man looked over his shoulder, Micah recognized the guest that had paid Laney too much attention at lunch. He'd wanted to rip the guy's throat out earlier, but now he had an excuse. He was defending his home and his heart now, and he wasn't going down without a fight.

Just as the man lunged into the back seat with Laney, Micah gripped two fists full of the man's coat and jerked him out onto the ground where he landed on his side.

The truck engine roared to life, and Micah grabbed for the door handle on the front passenger seat. Forgetting the man on the ground, he dove across the front seat at the man in the driver's seat.

In the dim light, Micah saw the man's fear written on his face. Good. He hoped the guy knew who was coming for him.

Micah grabbed the man past his flailing arms and dragged him through the truck and out the other side before throwing him on the ground where the other guy was getting to his feet.

The first guy was bending, getting ready to tackle Micah, and he knew those years of high school football were about to pay off. Micah met him head on and laid the guy out again.

They both landed hard, but Micah quickly restrained the other man beneath him. With the full advantage, Micah let his fist fly. The first impact was powerful and satisfying as his knuckles collided with the man's face. The second punch packed just as much force, but Micah felt the shock through his hand.

"Micah!" Laney screamed behind him.

He turned just as a fist collided with his own face. The pain was dulled by his adrenaline, and Micah snapped his attention back to the assailant. Pushing to his feet, Micah returned the blow instantly, sending the guy flying backward to the ground.

A new light shone from near the other headlights, and Micah's brother Aaron jumped from his truck.

Micah had been fending off both men on his own, but he sagged in relief at the sight of backup. He turned to where Laney staggered from the back seat of the truck and ran to her, wrapping an arm around her middle to help her balance.

"Laney! Are you okay?" He pushed her hair from her face, examining her for injuries.

Her eyes widened, fixed on something behind him. At her warning, he turned just as the man he'd pulled from the driver's seat pulled back a fist.

Before he let the hand fly, Aaron crashed into him, sending both of them to the ground.

Aaron shuffled to his knees, pinning the other man beneath him. "There's a rope in the back seat of my truck," he yelled over his shoulder.

Micah searched the area for the guest that attacked Laney. The man lay unconscious a few feet away.

Assured that the threat was gone, Micah turned back to Laney. "I'll be right back. Are you okay for a minute?"

She nodded emphatically. "I'm fine. Go." She rested a hand against the side of her head and leaned back against the stranger's truck.

Micah rushed to Aaron's truck and fumbled through tools in the back seat. He found the rope and two wrenches. He wished he'd thought to grab a weapon earlier.

When Micah returned, Aaron was still wrestling with the man beneath him.

When the stranger saw the rope, his panic surged. "No! No!"

Aaron and Micah fought to restrain the man's wrists together as he continued to thrash.

"Laney! Laney!" the man's voice was hoarse as he yelled.

In that moment, Micah knew he'd been wrestling against Devin. The man was foolish enough to come to Micah's door, and he didn't feel sorry for the fate that awaited the scumbag.

A siren pierced the air, and Devin fought harder against the ropes around his wrists and against Aaron as he held him down.

Laney leaned against the side of the truck where he'd left her. Her hand covered her mouth as red and blue lights flashed across her face. She stared at the man restrained on the ground.

Micah returned to her side. "Laney, are you hurt?"

"No. I'm fine. Just... scared. Glad it's over." As if pulled from a trance, she looked around at the scene.

The remaining guests huddled in the open doorway of the main house watching the commotion outside. Asa emerged from his patrol vehicle as two other police cars parked nearby.

Micah pulled her into his arms, and she clung to him instantly. He felt the sobs shaking her body as he held her. She'd been through so much, and now this. Would she ever feel safe again?

"I'm so sorry." Her words were garbled and hoarse. "I put everyone in danger."

Micah rubbed a hand over her hair. "No. It's not your fault. Laney, you didn't do this."

Her voice was high and shrill as she screamed, "They were here for me. I'm sorry!"

"Laney, listen to me." Micah pulled her away so she could see the sincerity in his eyes. "I'm not afraid of any man. The only thing that scares me is losing you." He pressed a quick and hard kiss against her forehead. "I will always protect you. Do you understand?"

She squeezed her eyes closed, and her sobs intensified. Micah pulled her close again and held her against his chest until the police had taken control of the two men who'd attacked Laney. He wasn't sure how long they stood there, but he would happily hold her here, protected from the dangers of the world, as long as she'd let him.

CHAPTER 22

LANEY

Laney was exhausted by the time everyone had given their statements and the police left, but there were a million more questions to be answered as the family members returned from the Lawrence farm. Micah hadn't left her side, and the Hardings comforted her in different ways. To have narrowly escaped danger, she felt oddly safe surrounded by these people who would rush to her aid at a moment's notice.

She'd tried to properly thank Aaron, but her words fell flat. He'd risked so much, and without knowing anything about the situation, he'd jumped in to help.

Finally, Micah announced that he was taking Laney home, and she silently thanked the Lord for the wonderful man beside her. She would be who knew where tonight without him, and now he was whisking her away from the aftermath.

When Micah parked the truck in front of Laney's cabin and shut off the engine, he turned to her. "Would you mind if I sleep on the couch? I really don't want to be far from you tonight."

The vulnerability in his words pierced her heart. She'd feared for her own life tonight, but the experience had impacted Micah just as deeply. "Of course."

They stepped into the cabin together, and Micah scanned the small space as he closed the door behind them.

"I don't think we have anything to worry about anymore," she said. "The police have Devin."

Micah's gaze landed on her. "I know. I'm still amped up from everything that happened."

Exhaustion and worry filled his features, and she wrapped her arms around his waist. "It's over now. You can relax."

He brushed a hand over her hair and rested his cheek against her head. "I know. Let's get some sleep."

She pulled away and sighed. "Yeah, I'm not going to be worth much in the morning."

"Don't worry about it. We'll sleep in."

Laney slipped into the bedroom to change clothes. When she tiptoed back into the living room, Micah was laid out on the couch. His boots were lined up beside the door, and he'd taken off his flannel shirt, leaving a gray thermal undershirt. He could have walked thirty steps to his own cabin and changed clothes, but judging by his alertness when she entered the room, it didn't look like he was leaving anytime soon.

She grabbed an extra blanket and pillow from the small closet and handed them to him. "I feel bad you're sleeping on the couch."

"I'm fine. I've slept in worse places." The playful half-grin he flashed assured her of his sincerity.

"Did Asa say anything about who the other guy might be?" she asked.

Micah shrugged. "I haven't talked to him since he left. It looked like he had his hands full."

"Okay. I just wonder how he knew Devin."

Micah sat up on the couch and reached for her hand. He tugged her closer until she sat on the cushion beside him. "Trust me. I won't stop until I have all the answers."

"I know," she whispered.

His gaze swept over her face, from her hairline to her chin and back up, searching for bumps or scratches. When he was satisfied that nothing had marred her this time, he cradled the side of her face with his strong hand.

"I love you, Laney. I couldn't take it if anything happened to you."

Air rushed from her lungs. His declaration of

love was shocking, but it also wasn't. Hadn't he shown her his love in different ways for months now? His constant attention to her, taking her home every evening, his tender touches and longing gazes. He asked about her day, if she slept well, if she needed anything.

She did need something. She needed Micah. And he'd already given her the greatest gift. He would be the first and last person she gave her whole heart to. He would respect her, he would cherish her, and he would keep the Lord at the forefront of their relationship.

"I love you too." The words were simple and true, and she felt the bonds that shackled her to her old life fall away.

He swept her into a slow and adoring kiss that sealed the words they'd spoken—to love each other without faltering for the rest of their lives.

Micah pulled away to rest his forehead against hers. "You've made me see that some things are more important than my job. *You* are more important. Every day, through the good and the bad. I want to be beside you."

Laney felt her eyes filling with moisture. Happy tears? Those were a real thing. "I want that too— being beside you every day."

His hand slid from the back of her neck to her cheek. "I'll put myself between you and danger any day. I'd give my last breath to save you. But I hope I never have to do those things and we can live a quiet life without danger. In the good times and the bad, I don't want you to ever doubt how much I love you." His calloused thumb moved gently over her jaw. "You're everything to me."

She rested her head on his shoulder. What a relief it was to begin and end the day with Micah by her side. They stayed there, resting in each other's arms, until she yawned, almost asleep from the comfort he provided.

"Get some rest." He kissed the top of her head and yawned. "I've had enough excitement for one day."

Laney chuckled. "Me too. Let's not do that again."

She kissed him good night and padded off to the bedroom. Sliding beneath the covers, she instantly fell into a sound sleep knowing Micah was close by.

The alarm shrieked, and Laney flung her arms toward the offending noise. She'd forgotten to disable the alarm, and six in the morning came early after getting in bed after midnight.

When the wake-up call was silenced, Laney rolled over and sighed. She'd never been able to fall back asleep after being woken up, but she didn't want to disturb Micah. One of them should get to rest.

She rolled over and grabbed the Bible beside her bed and began reading. There were notes and references in the margins and between chapters, and she made sure to read everything, taking in as much as she could. She'd accepted the Lord as her Savior just last week, and she was hungry for knowledge. There was so much left to learn.

After forty-five minutes of reading, she started to squirm. She needed to use the bathroom, but she was trying not to wake Micah.

When she couldn't take it any longer, she slipped out of her bedroom and into the bathroom. Minutes later, she tried to be just as sneaky when she crept out of the bathroom.

"Hey," Micah groaned.

Laney's shoulders slumped. "I didn't mean to wake you."

"No problem. You sleep okay?" He rubbed his eyes and then sat up to stretch.

She'd slept better than she could ever remember thanks to him. "Great. What about you?"

"Pretty good." He leaned to rest his elbows on his knees.

"You want some coffee?" she asked.

"I'd love some." He rose and followed her to the kitchen.

He sat at the table while she filled the coffee pot. When she turned around to wait for the coffee to brew, Micah's expression caught her off guard. It was a mixture of indecision and apprehension. A faint bruise was forming on his right cheek from the one punch Devin had gotten in last night.

"Is everything okay?" she hesitantly asked. She almost hadn't asked at all in the hope that the foreboding feeling that crept up her spine would go away.

"I think so," Micah said, looking down at his hands on the table. "I have something to ask you about."

"Okay." She drug the word out, unsure if she wanted to step into this conversation that made Micah so uneasy.

"You might want to sit," he said.

Oh, boy. This wasn't good. Her nerves felt like guitar strings, pulled taut and strummed, vibrating endlessly. She eased into the chair across from him.

"Asa called me yesterday. He said someone named Colton Erwin in Laramie County filed a police report about an employee who had stolen a lot of money from his business."

"That's Devin's brother," Laney said as she sat up straighter.

"I figured. He put your name in the police report as a suspect."

"He thinks I stole from him?" Laney shrieked. That was ridiculous. She'd been so careful with every penny the bar brought in, and she'd always been open with him about everything she did.

Micah reached out a hand to cover hers. "I don't know anything else, but I think Asa can help us figure out what's going on. Would Colton and Devin try to frame you for something like this?"

"I promise I didn't take any money from him or anyone," Laney said quickly. "Every cent was accounted for. I kept detailed records—"

"Laney, slow down." He cradled her face in his large hands to try to calm her. "I don't think you did it. Even before you said so yourself, I didn't think you'd actually taken any money."

"I didn't. I would never..." It was becoming hard to breathe as the implications settled on her shoulders.

"Stop. I know. Take a deep breath."

Laney sucked in a breath. Micah believed her. Everything would be okay as long as Micah believed her.

No one had ever believed in her before.

Micah picked up her hand and held it between both of his own. "Now, we have to figure out what's going on. Asa thinks we should get in front of this and address it head on."

"How?" her voice was barely above a whisper.

"Talk to Colton."

Her gaze landed on their linked hands as she thought about his suggestion. "You mean, go to the bar?" She'd been so adamant that she wouldn't ever set foot in that place again. Now, she'd have to go back willingly.

"Let's get the information and figure out why he thinks you would have taken money. It might have something to do with the reason Devin kept hounding you."

Laney tilted her head to the side. "You make it sound so simple."

"I hope it can be," Micah said. "But I'll be right beside you no matter what."

CHAPTER 23

MICAH

"That's it," Laney said as she pointed to the old wooden building off the side of the road.

Surrounded by a gravel lot, Dive In didn't look like anything to write home about. Maybe that was the allure of a local bar—off on its own and miles from anyone who might complain about the noise or rowdy drunkards. The bright midday sun shone on the worn roof and rotting doorframes.

"It kind of looks like I expected," Micah said as the tires crunched over the gravel parking lot.

When they parked and Micah killed the engine, Laney stared at the entrance.

"Hey, there's nothing to worry about." He picked up her hand where she was twisting her fingers and lifted it to his lips, placing a kiss on the back. "We're just here to talk. I'm right beside you."

She smiled and squeezed his hand. "I know he

won't hurt me. At least he won't as long as you're around. I don't know much about Colton. He wasn't a part of the daily operations. I've only met him twice."

"Don't worry. I'll take care of him. Let's get this over with." Micah ran around the front of the truck to open Laney's door and held her hand as they walked inside.

The bar was empty as Colton had assured them it would be. He'd agreed to meet with them privately before opening hours, and he hadn't seemed too worked up when Micah had called him to arrange the meeting.

A tall, thin man stepped from an open doorway in the back of the bar. His dark hair was cut short, and he wore a collared shirt and jeans.

Micah tightened his grip on Laney's hand, letting her know he wasn't leaving her side.

"Mr. Harding." The man extended a hand to Micah. "Colton Erwin. Thanks for coming."

Micah took the offered hand and gave it a firm shake. "Thanks for agreeing to meet with us."

Colton turned to Laney. "It's good to see you again, Laney." He extended his hand to her.

"You too." She shook the hand, but kept her other hand entwined with Micah's.

Colton looked back and forth between Micah and Laney. "I think this is all a misunderstanding. I've learned some things since I filed that police report. Come on over here, and I'll show you." He gestured toward a table where a laptop sat open and stacks of papers covered most of the area.

Micah and Laney sat as Colton picked up a short stack of what looked like invoices. "These are monthly bills from a company called United Alliance dating back over two years. The amount is the same on each invoice, and the only thing that changes is the due date. Do these look familiar?"

Laney reached for the stack and flipped through them. "Yes. I paid them every month."

"It seems you did—with a credit card online," Colton said.

"That's how Devin told me to pay them."

"I assumed. See, after you left, I came back to help out with the business side until we could find a replacement for you. I haven't worked alongside Devin in years, but he always seemed to have things covered here. When I got here, he was adamant that he didn't need my help. He kept trying to push me out of the office, but I refused to let the bills go unpaid. My name is on this business just as much as his. When he finally got aggressive about keeping me out of the finances, I knew he was hiding something.

"When I first discovered these monthly charges, I thought you had been depositing the money into your own account. That's when I filed the police report."

Laney sat up straighter. "I never took any money."

"I know," Colton quickly assured her. "I know that now. You see, after Devin was arrested and I found out what he'd done to you, I checked his laptop. I found the template and letterhead for United Alliance. He created these fake invoices every month and had you pay them. The money went into his account."

Laney stared at the stack of invoices. "That was thousands of dollars." She covered her mouth with her hand.

"As soon as Micah called me about you, I knew you hadn't been a part of this. Devin has always pushed the limits of honesty, and I'm not completely surprised he did this." Colton rubbed his chin and sighed. "I should have been more involved in the business or gotten out of it altogether. I don't have any desire to own and operate this place."

"I'm so sorry about all of this," Laney said. "I had no idea. I can't believe I did this. I never would have had I known."

Colton held up a hand to halt her apology. "I believe you. When I heard about Devin's assault and the police department told me about his obsessive attempts to contact you, I put the pieces together. I'm sure this is why he wanted you to come back. He wanted to keep getting those deposits without having to put his hands directly in the act. He'd have a hard time explaining this to a new hire."

"It makes sense. He really just used me all these years."

"When he couldn't find you, he hired a private investigator. We've known Brett Caldwell since we were kids, and I wasn't surprised to hear he'd been a part of this."

Laney shook her head. "I can't believe he did this. What was he going to do, kidnap me and force me to continue working here?"

"I have no idea. My guess is he might have offered you a piece of the pot to keep doing what you'd been doing all these years." Colton rapped his knuckles on the table. "Well, I wanted you to know that I'll be contacting the police department about the new information. I'll clear your name and let them know you're not responsible for this."

"Will you get your money back?" Laney asked.

Colton shrugged. "I have no idea, but that isn't your problem to worry about. I'm hiring a new bookkeeper for now, and you left excellent records of everything. It shouldn't be hard for someone to step in and keep things running. After that, I think I'm going to get rid of this place. I'd like to sell it. I don't live here, and I'm ready to let it go. I was in a different place in my life when I thought owning a bar was a good idea."

"I understand," Laney said. "I'm in a different

place in my life now than I was when I worked here. None of that is your fault, but I'm so glad to be where I am now."

Colton grinned. "I can see that. I'm glad you have someone looking out for you. I'm sure Devin didn't."

Laney's eyes widened in agreement. "You'd be correct."

"I'm sorry for anything he did to you. I know he's a grown man, and I'm not responsible for his actions, but I hate that he mistreated you."

Laney handed the stack of incriminating invoices back to him. "It's over now. I'm where I'm supposed to be."

Colton stood. "It's been a pleasure meeting with you. Laney, always good to see you again."

"Thank you for clearing everything up. I'm glad we got some closure," Micah said as he stood to his feet.

"I hope you're able to get your money back. I'm really sorry for the part I played in this," Laney said.

"I would never blame you. You were tricked just like I was." Colton gestured to the bar. "Let me get you some water for the road. You have a long drive back north."

He returned with the drinks, and they all said their good-byes. When Micah and Laney stepped back into the bright parking lot, he released a tired sigh.

"I don't know about you, but I hope I never see this place again," Micah said.

"You and me both. I think we're finished here." Laney rested her head against his shoulder as they walked back to the truck.

Micah opened the passenger door, and he waited until Laney was settled in her seat before closing it. He couldn't wait to leave this place with Laney. It held so many bad memories for her, and he wanted only good memories for her in the future.

When he took his place behind the steering wheel, he snuck a glance at Laney. "Where to?"

"I could go for a puff pastry," Laney said.

"Point me toward the closest bakery," Micah said as he started the engine.

"Then, I'd like to go home," she added.

Warmth filled his chest at the innocence of her request. Laney wanted a home, and he would do anything to give her the best home he could for the rest of his life.

"Home it is."

EPILOGUE
LANEY

"Are these ready?" Laney asked as she picked up the bowl of warm biscuits.

"Yep. Ready to go." Haley slid the baking sheet into the sink filled with dirty pans and dishes.

Laney grabbed the tongs and a dish towel as she hurried from the kitchen into the meeting room. The largest room in the main house was bustling with chatter and laughter as the Hardings and guests stood around in small groups talking of everything from horse trails to the coming end of the summer season.

Three months had passed since Devin's arrest, and she'd come to love her new life at Blackwater Ranch. She didn't have to look over her shoulder or spend every day praying Devin wouldn't find her.

The Lawrence family had yet to overcome the loss of their matriarch, and Mama Harding still spent many hours with the neighbors. Like today, when she left Laney and Haley to prepare and serve breakfast for the family, workers, and guests of the ranch.

Laney set the bowl on the serving counter and turned to face the room full of smiling faces. "Okay, everyone!" she yelled to be heard over the dozens of voices. "Guests first!"

The bed and breakfast was rapidly growing. Thankfully, the guests who'd witnessed part of Devin's attempted abduction had been understanding. They'd shown support and opened their arms to help instead of leaving scathing reviews on travel sites.

Strong arms wound around her waist from behind, and she leaned back into Micah's warm embrace. "Good morning."

"Good morning." He kissed her temple before hugging her tight.

"Big plans today?" she asked.

"Pretty big."

Laney rolled her eyes. "Let me guess. Hay needs baling. Big plans."

"Ha-ha. You think you're funny." Micah narrowed his eyes, but the corners of his mouth turned up.

"I mean, I can usually guess." She playfully ticked off the items on her fingers. "A fence needs fixing, a tractor needs fixing, cows need to be fed. It's the same ol' same ol'."

Micah's grin stretched. "Yep. Same ol' same ol'." He kissed her forehead and grabbed her hand. "Let's eat."

The guests were a flurry of excitement all through the meal. Half of them were spending the day with Lucas and Maddie on a trail ride, and the other half were going fishing with Noah and Camille. The appeal of the Blackwater Ranch Bed and Breakfast was the immersive experience into the daily work that kept the place running, and the guests seemed to love it.

Levi, the ranch's biggest promoter, told stories of the things the guests could expect while out on the ranch each day. The little boy would start school soon, and the Hardings weren't ready to see their littlest worker go. He was the first one up and the first one to volunteer to help despite being only four years old.

Laney watched the kid with a longing in her heart. Levi brought so much happiness to the ranch, and she hoped one day she and Micah could raise a child in this loving family.

He hadn't proposed yet, but she knew in her heart that they were heading in that direction. She may joke about the monotony of his ranch duties, but she wouldn't trade the hard-working man beside her for anything. In fact, she admired his commitment to his family and the life they'd built here.

Jameson had been hired full-time not long ago, and Micah had learned to delegate. He still worked all hours of the day, but he made time to spend with Laney. It meant much more than any gift he could have given her.

She had once thought Micah had rescued her from the shackles of the terrible life she'd been living, but now she knew the truth. Micah's kindness came from above. He'd been doing the work of the Savior when he took in a poor stranger.

Micah had saved her, but not in the way she'd expected. He led her to Christ, the One who would be with her every step of the way. Micah had given her a Heavenly Father and a family overflowing with love like she'd never known.

She looked around and marveled at the abundance of love, food, and friendship. What more could she ever want?

Micah stood from his seat next to her, and everyone in the room quieted.

Levi yelled, "Yes! It's time!"

A round of chuckles filled the room, and Laney looked questioningly at Micah. Everyone knew something she didn't.

Micah turned to her and slid his hand into hers. "Laney Parker."

When he said her name with reverence, she

knew what was coming. Her chest grew tight with emotion, and she inhaled a long breath. She looked at the faces surrounding her. They all wore expressions of hope, excitement, and joy.

At the end of the table, Mama Harding stood next to Silas, her fist tucked under her chin with a knowing smile.

Micah knelt in front of her, his strong hand holding hers. There wasn't a hint of nervousness as he held his shoulders back. He was a man sure of every movement, every word as he looked up at her.

"Laney, I want you by my side. I want to call you my bride, my wife, and my helpmate. You're the love of my life."

She swallowed hard, but there was no keeping the tears at bay. Happiness filled her up, and it needed a way out—a way to express the joy that pushed at her ribcage, begging to be set free.

After a lifetime of being talked down to and beaten with words, Micah called her worthy and loved.

"I want to give you a life of happiness and love." He pulled a golden ring from his pocket and held it out to her. "Will you marry me?"

Laney nodded until she could speak. "Yes."

Micah stood to wrap her in his arms. As he held her tight, she fought to catch her breath. Cheers and whistles roared in her ears, but she heard Micah's whispered words above them all.

"I love you. Don't forget it. I'll be loving you until the day I die."

"I love you too." They were the easiest words she'd ever spoken, and they marked the beginning of the rest of her life at Blackwater Ranch.

BONUS EPILOGUE
AARON

Aaron stared at the computer screen. The letters began running together after reading the eleventh email, and now he couldn't make sense out of the words.

Camille reached a hand over his shoulder and pointed at the top of the resume. "She misspelled objective."

"You've found something wrong with every resume," Aaron said.

"And we'll keep looking until we find the right one," Camille said. "How can we trust this person to teach Levi if she can't use spellcheck?"

Fair enough. Aaron closed the document and clicked on the next email.

He hated computers, mostly because he didn't know how to do anything beyond turning them on or off. He could handle just about anything on the ranch except the computer. At least not without Camille or Laney's help.

"This one looks okay," Laney said as she leaned over Aaron's other shoulder.

Camille pointed at the bottom of the email. "Nope, she can only work 8:00 AM to 2:00 PM."

Laney sang, "Next."

Aaron clicked to the next email. He'd posted the job opening for a nanny two months ago, and so far, the applicants hadn't been promising.

Aaron had made the decision to homeschool his son, at least for the first year. Levi was smart for his age, and he loved the ranch. Tearing him away from this place for seven hours a day would be a tough transition. If he had the option to stay here with someone who could give him a one-on-one learning experience, they could have the best of both worlds.

"Oh, this one sounds sweet," Laney said.

"How do you know what she sounds like?" Aaron asked.

"I don't know. The tone of her email."

Camille hummed as she continued to read. "She does seem nice."

Aaron tried to read the words, but he was having a hard time focusing. He prayed he hadn't passed his short attention span to Levi.

"She said she's interested in the on-site housing," Camille said.

"That would be super convenient," Laney said.

Hearing the ember of hope in Camille's voice, Aaron willed his gaze to focus on the words in the email.

I love children.

The ranch sounds wonderful.

I could start immediately.

Aaron continued to read the words that buoyed his hopes.

Camille ran the pendant of her necklace along the chain as she stared at the screen. "Wow. She has five years of experience with the Wyoming home-school system, and she has some impressive certifications." She pointed at the screen again. "She homeschooled her nieces and nephews."

Aaron finished reading the resume—the one describing the person who seemed ideal for the job—and looked over his shoulder at Camille. "What's the catch?"

"She might not be as perfect in person as she seems on paper," Camille said.

"So, we get her in for an interview?" Aaron rested his chin in his hand and scratched his jaw.

"I think that's a good idea," Laney said.

"What if she gets here and Levi doesn't like her?" Aaron asked.

Laney patted his shoulder. "We'll cross that bridge when we come to it."

The black letters on the white screen blurred.

Aaron sighed and rested his head in his hands. He never expected the search for a nanny who could also teach his son *and* be willing to relocate to be so stressful. Maybe he was asking too much. But the pay he'd offer was generous. He'd gladly pay top dollar so Levi could be happy.

He wanted his son to enjoy learning. Aaron remembered the years he'd struggled through school. He wanted learning to be easier for Levi.

Camille clapped her hands as if inciting motivation in a group of teenagers. It reminded Aaron of his high school football coach during their half-time pep talks. "Hey, I don't want to hear your bellyaching."

Aaron held up his hands. "I didn't even say anything!"

"I can hear it in your exaggerated sigh. Levi needs this, and so do you."

Aaron wanted peace of mind. He wanted to be able to work the ranch every day knowing Levi was taken care of, learning, and having fun being a kid.

He turned the chair around to face the women. "I can't believe we're actually considering hiring a stranger off the internet." He had no idea what the internet actually looked like, but he had a vision of lots of wires and numbers.

Laney thumped him in the forehead. "I ended up here because of a job posting on the internet."

Reminded of his big mouth, he carefully put his foot in it. "Sorry. I forgot. This is important to me. I want Levi to be smart."

"And he will be," Laney said. "He's already smart for his age. I don't think you have anything to worry about. That kid is like a sponge."

Camille nodded. "Yep. Don't worry. If we can't find anyone that's the right fit to homeschool him, we'll move to plan B."

"What's plan B?" Aaron asked.

Camille shrugged. "I don't know. We haven't talked about it yet."

The closest school was a short haul toward Blackwater, but with the ranch expanding and the bed and breakfast booming, it would be hard to find someone who could stop in the middle of the day to go get him.

"Hey, I said no worrying. Turn that frown upside down," Camille commanded, pointing and circling his face in the air with her finger.

"She's right," Laney said. "Levi has a dozen people right here who teach him things every day. We know he can learn, and he'll do fine once he gets in school."

"Don't worry. We'll find the perfect teacher for him," Camille said.

Aaron rubbed at his chest. Why was it so hard to think about his boy starting school? He'd never been away from Levi for more than a few hours. Hopefully, he would be the only one with attachment issues. Levi was a champ at adapting to new situations. He certainly hadn't gotten that from his mother.

Now was not the time to think about Levi's mother. In fact, he was better off forgetting about her.

It was for the best. Aaron didn't know what to think about her. He thought he'd loved her at one point. If he wasn't sure, it was a pretty good sign that it hadn't really been love when she left them. She'd given him his son, the best part of his life, but no matter how hard he tried, he couldn't make it work with her.

Still, he wished Levi had a mother—a woman in his life who could make the best decisions for him. All Aaron knew was ranching, and some days it felt like Levi was getting shortchanged in the parent department.

Camille crossed her arms and tapped her foot. "Are you going to call her or what?"

Aaron turned back to the resume on the screen. What would she be like? She looked perfect on paper, but he was keenly aware that the higher his hopes rose, the further he had to fall if this didn't work out. He wanted to hope that she was the one. If Levi liked her, this might actually work.

Camille shoved Aaron's shoulder in rhythm with her chant, "Do it. Do it. Do it."

Willing his hand not to shake as he picked up the phone, Aaron dialed the number and prayed this woman was the answer to his prayers.

OTHER BOOKS BY MANDI BLAKE

Blackwater Ranch Series
Complete Contemporary Western Romance Series
Remembering the Cowboy
Charmed by the Cowboy
Mistaking the Cowboy
Protected by the Cowboy
Keeping the Cowboy
Redeeming the Cowboy

Blackwater Ranch Series Box Set 1-3
Blackwater Ranch Series Box Set 4-6
Blackwater Ranch Complete Series Box Set

Wolf Creek Ranch Series
Complete Contemporary Western Romance Series
Truth is a Whisper
Almost Everything

The Only Exception
Better Together
The Other Side
Forever After All

Love in Blackwater Series
Small Town Series
Love in the Storm
Love for a Lifetime

Unfailing Love Series
Complete Small-Town Christian Romance Series
A Thousand Words
Just as I Am
Never Say Goodbye
Living Hope
Beautiful Storm
All the Stars
What if I Loved You

Unfailing Love Series Box Set 1-3
Unfailing Love Series Box Set 4-6
Unfailing Love Complete Series Box Set

Heroes of Freedom Ridge Series
Multi-Author Christmas Series
Rescued by the Hero
Guarded by the Hero
Hope for the Hero

Christmas in Redemption Ridge Series
Multi-Author Christmas Series
Dreaming About Forever

Blushing Brides Series
Multi-Author Series
The Billionaire's Destined Bride

About the Author

Mandi Blake was born and raised in Alabama where she lives with her husband and daughter, but her southern heart loves to travel. Reading has been her favorite hobby for as long as she can remember, but writing is her passion. She loves a good happily ever after in her sweet Christian romance books and loves to see her characters' relationships grow closer to God and each other.

Acknowledgments

I'm incredibly grateful to have so many people who support me and encourage me to write. I absolutely love what I do, but I couldn't do it alone.

Thanks to my beta readers, Jenna Eleam, Pam Humphrey, Tanya Smith, and Kendra Haneline. They are the best at pointing out my errors and steering the story in the right direction.

I'm blessed to have a family who believes in me. I couldn't do it without them. My husband makes sure I have time to write, my daughter thinks it's so cool that I write books, my sister, Kenda Goforth, is my biggest fan, and my mom reads all of my books, even though I know she doesn't enjoy reading.

I independently publish all of my books, but that doesn't mean I do it alone. My cover designer, Amanda Walker, is incredibly good at graphic design. I don't know the first thing about fonts, and she saves me on a regular basis. My sweet editor, Brandi Aquino, does so much for these books, and I appreciate her hard work.

I also want to thank you for reading this book.

I've made so many reader friends since I began publishing, and I'm thankful for every time our paths cross. I was an avid reader before I was a writer, and I appreciate the time you take to read the stories I love so much.

KEEPING THE COWBOY

BLACKWATER RANCH BOOK 5

When her dreams become a reality, will she be able to leave the family she's come to love?

Jade Smith has always dreamed of teaching abroad. While she waits for her chance, she takes a nannying position at Blackwater Ranch. It's supposed to be temporary, but she soon learns that this devoted single dad and his boisterous five-year-old won't be easy to leave when the time comes.

Aaron Harding was wrecked when his ex bailed on him and their son, leaving him to raise Levi alone. He's in no hurry for either of them to fall in love again. It just isn't worth the risk. But as he watches the way Jade cares for his son, he starts to wonder if a happy, two-parent family is finally within their reach.

When the opportunity of a lifetime leaves Jade

with an impossible decision to make, will she choose to follow the dreams of her past or to make this man and his son her future?

Made in the USA
Coppell, TX
30 July 2024

35337613R00173